I0601463

KISS ME BY MOONLIGHT

MICHELE ZURLO

OMNIFIC PUBLISHING
LOS ANGELES

Kiss Me by Moonlight, Copyright © Michele Zurlo, 2014
All Rights Reserved. Except as permitted under the U.S. Copyright Act of 1976,
no part of this publication may be reproduced, distributed, or transmitted
in any form or by any means, or stored in a database or retrieval system,
without prior written permission of the publisher.

Omnific Publishing
1901 Avenue of the Stars, 2nd floor
Los Angeles, CA 90067
www.omnificpublishing.com

First Omnific eBook edition, June 2014
First Omnific trade paperback edition, June 2014

The characters and events in this book are fictitious.
Any similarity to real persons, living or dead,
is coincidental and not intended by the author.

Library of Congress Cataloguing-in-Publication Data

Zurlo, Michele.
  Kiss Me by Moonlight / Michele Zurlo – 1st ed.
  ISBN: 978-1-623421-19-9
  1. Contemporary Romance — Fiction. 2. Detroit — Fiction.
  3. OCD — Fiction. 4. Childhood Trauma — Fiction. I. Title

10 9 8 7 6 5 4 3 2 1

Cover Design by Micha Stone and Amy Brokaw
Interior Book Design by Coreen Montagna

Printed in the United States of America

*For Twin #1
who has lots of insightful advice and wisdom beyond her years*

Prologue...Sort of

Hey there! If you're reading this, you must be interested in what happened with Dylan and me after I landed them a spot opening for AFI and helped them sign a recording contract. Luma said you would be. And Jane concurred, which is the only reason I'm writing this. They made me do it.

Plus, you probably saw the online gossip headlines or the #man-whore Twitter feed.

If you're scratching your head in bewilderment, you need to go back and read *Kiss Me Goodnight*. This book really only tells the second part of our story, though if you want to take your chances, that's fine too. I've made a lot of really bad decisions in my life, so who am I to judge? Just don't be surprised to find out I'm messed up and I say things I shouldn't. You'll find yourself shouting at me and throwing down your book in disgust without fully understanding why I do the things I do—not that I'm excusing my behavior. Excuses don't often excuse anything, and nobody knows this better than I.

Anyway, I hope things have gone well for you since last we met. I wish I could say the same for me, but then I'd be living somebody else's life, and you wouldn't be reading my story.

For what it's worth, I hope you not only enjoy my tale, but learn some things about Dylan and me that didn't rate media attention.

Welcome back.

Chapter One

"Lacey? Have you seen my shoes?"

I was in the bathroom, toweling my hair dry. I'd been growing it out for the past few months — mostly because there hadn't been time to make it to the salon — and soon I was either going to fall in love with it or sharpen scissors for a frustrated massacre. I've cut my own hair a few times, and although my mother always laughs as she recounts my rather impressive childhood attempts, later in life, it hasn't gone well. Anyway, Dylan's question nearly put me over the edge, but I took a deep breath, adjusted the towel covering my nakedness, and got myself under control. "Which ones?"

"Converse high tops. The blue ones with the TARDIS windows painted on them."

He'd ordered those from a British company after seeing a picture of them online. My alt-rock boyfriend has a geek streak. He also has about twelve other pairs of shoes floating around my apartment. No man should own that much footwear. Call me sexist, but if the closet is going to be full of shoes, they should be my shoes. Men only need two pair: regular and dress.

He came into the bathroom, where I had the drawer open that houses the nail scissors. I was contemplating hairicide, not the location of his shoes.

"Lace?"

I sighed. "I threw them out."

"Really?" He didn't bat a lash.

"No."

"Look, I know you're stressed, but I am too. I can't do this right now."

He's referring to sorting through the morass of my lies. In the past four months since we've become a couple, he's become adept at reading me. For my part, I've put my efforts to stop lying on hold. Too much upheaval in my life makes it nearly impossible. It feels good to lie, and I need those small pleasures.

Usually I only lie to Dylan—or about him. Small lies, to his sister or bandmates. I blame bruises and small cuts on him, which is ironic because I freak out at the sight of blood, so Dylan is usually the one bandaging wherever I've been cut. However, some of my injuries *are* actually his fault. He likes to throw me onto the bed, and sometimes we get rather rough between the sheets. I cooperate and participate enthusiastically, so don't get the wrong impression. It's funny how circumstances change. When Dylan pledged his love to me, I don't think he understood the type of carnival ride our relationship would be. And for all intents and purposes, he's my first true boyfriend, so neither did I.

This morning's interaction is typical for us. I don't know why, but he likes to ask me where his things are. My apartment is small; it isn't difficult to find things. Here's a sample conversation:

Dylan: Lacey, have you seen my sunglasses?

Me: They were on top of your head the last time I saw them.

Dylan: Really?

Me: No. Check the junk drawer in the kitchen.

Note that even my junk drawer, the place where people throw shit they didn't know where else to put, has items in multiples of six. He knows it bothers me that he doesn't follow this unwritten rule, yet he doesn't make an effort to accommodate my OCD quirks.

So, he'll check the drawer, and there they are. I know he knows I put them there, because they're nestled with five other pairs, yet I can't just tell him where I put them. This frustrates him, which gives me a secret thrill. I'm being passive-aggressive (for reasons I'll explain shortly), and he's putting up with it. In his position, I would take my twelve pairs of shoes and move back in with my sister. I'd still date me, but I wouldn't put this address on my driver's license.

"Shoes, Lacey. Have you seen them?"

I shook my head, also another lie. Though I couldn't remember exactly where he'd stowed them, I had a vivid memory of the mail carrier ringing my bell to deliver the package. It happened six days ago, and it annoyed the hell out of me. You see, Dylan having his mail delivered to my apartment is a sore spot, one that makes me not care too much if he finds the shoes. Call me crazy, but I think you should actually live someplace before you change your mailing address.

"Will you help me look?"

"Dylan, it's a radio interview. They're not going to be checking out your shoes. Why can't you wear one of the other dozen pairs sitting by the front door that I trip over whenever I come home?"

Oh, yes—I went there. I nagged. It isn't a romantic or new-girlfriend-y thing to say, but I don't care. Two words, Dylan: hall closet.

"I want to wear the TARDIS ones. They're good luck."

I refrained from growling. Dylan maintains—and it is a sweet sentiment—that we were fated to be together. The concepts of fate or destiny don't rate too high on my realism-o-meter. I've chalked our various pre-relationship encounters to coincidence. We happened to be in the same place at the same time on a couple of occasions. Isn't that how most people meet?

Did I mention that this shoe search is taking place at five o'clock on a Monday morning? And the band spent the weekend playing a string of shows in the Chicago area? We arrived home yesterday at seven, but I hadn't fallen into bed until eleven. I was exhausted. Yes, I was grouchy, but that wasn't my only complaint. I also might mention that he has yet to wear the shoes. How they qualify as good luck, I have no idea.

"Did you loan them to Monty?" His nephew has large feet, though he isn't quite to the point where Dylan's shoes fit him well. Monty thought the shoes were cool, so he'd hinted that he might "borrow" them and stuff the toe with tissue.

Dylan leaned against the jamb and blocked most of my exit. He's one of those handsome men who are tall with a lithe build.

For today's promotional adventure, he'd chosen to wear a Kiss Me Goodnight T-shirt I designed. It's black with white lettering. The pair of puckered lips I used to dot the i's are black as well. They reflect as shiny shapes on the shirt—subtle, but they look cool. The band isn't sold on this logo, but their label likes it more than the others the band proposed, so they've agreed to use it for their first album.

Whipcord muscles shifted and tensed as Dylan crossed his arms and seemed to think for a moment. "No. I was going to buy him a pair, but Daisy said to wait another month because he's in the middle of a growth spurt right now. Man, I remember when I was twelve. I shot up five inches that year."

When I met Monty, he was my height: five-foot-three. In the past two months, he'd left me in the dust. I don't know anything about Monty's biological father—and there's no way I'm comfortable enough to bring up the topic with Daisy—but I know Monty comes from tall stock on his mother's side. Dylan is five-eleven, and Daisy is almost that height. From photos I've seen of their parents, shortness isn't even a recessive trait.

I glanced in the mirror at my hair. The curls were drying. It was at the point where it was beginning to look nice. I hurried to smooth leave-in conditioner through it, hoping it would stay damp long enough so that if anybody took pictures, it wouldn't look too frizzy. Of course, they wouldn't be taking pictures of me, but I'd be right next to Dylan, so parts of me might show up. My mother loves to see photos of me in the media. I don't, but I'm growing used to it. Because not only am I Dylan's arm candy, I'm his band's manager.

"Have you looked under my bed?"

He glanced toward the bedroom, a mutinous slant to his mouth.

Yes, I said *my* bed. All of his things are here, this is where he sleeps, and I gave him my spare key. But I haven't put him on the lease or asked him to contribute to rent. He buys most of the food, but that's only fair since he eats most of it. I know he wants to officially move in, but I refuse to ask him. I simply am not ready to take that step. The fact that he has crept into my space like kudzu vine on the side of the freeway doesn't make me happy. I like having him around, but after moving so fucking slow for so long, he reversed speeds too quickly for my issue-laden mind to accept. Every lifeline I try to grasp has shattered as I wrestle with the ways our association has abruptly changed. Thinking about it makes me desperate, and that brings out my worst qualities, so I avoid thinking and go straight to my proven coping mechanisms.

Discussing the matter never has led anywhere good, so I felt confident he wouldn't bring up the issue right before we were scheduled to leave for the radio studio. Plus, I was visibly on edge, and I had been for several days. The (even) larger reason for my displeasure kept trying to batter my plans, so I squished it back down (again) and thought about what I had to do today.

"Our bed," he said after a moment.

And I'm wrong.

Nevertheless, I wasn't going to talk about it. That was small potatoes compared to the other thing. I turned away from him, sliding through the small space he'd left in the doorway so I could go look for the damn shoes myself. Dylan is king of the man-look, during which he can't find anything by himself, even if it's blinking neon lights in front of his eyes.

Snaking one arm out, he caught me around the waist before I could escape down the hall. I thought my body language was quite clear about not wanting to take on that topic, but Dylan must have been firmly in man-look territory. Either that, or his family counselor tendencies kicked in—he'd recently left his job as a therapist to pursue music full time—and he wasn't going to let me engage in avoidance behavior.

I stiffened.

"Lacey, look at me."

"Dylan, we need to get ready to go, and you can't find your shoes." I arched a superior brow at him, challenging him to make us late.

He crowded me against the wall. Though he didn't touch me, his magnetism held me in place. "You're not even dressed."

In point of fact, I wore only a towel, and it chose that moment to unravel and drop away. Dylan's gaze followed the path of newly exposed flesh. When he lifted it back to look in my eyes, the teal shade had darkened, and I knew we were going to be late.

I pushed at his chest. "Dylan, we don't have time. Let me find your shoes."

"Fuck the shoes." His lips closed over mine, a sudden and insistent attack that I'd never been able to resist. I was transported to that place where my thoughts drop away and I could only feel. I liked that place quite a bit, and he knew exactly how his kisses put me in a tailspin.

His hands roamed my still-damp skin, brushing fires that shot straight to my core. When his mouth broke away, I gasped for air. He kissed a path down my neck, sucking so hard I knew I was going to have a love bruise. I didn't care. I was too busy trying to keep my weakened knees from collapsing while the maelstrom of hormones he set loose inside my body ran riot.

He dropped to his knees and lifted my leg over his shoulder. From the reverent and hungry expression on his face, I knew I was in for one of Dylan's wild rides. He licked his lips, and then I felt his hot tongue where it counted.

This time when I said his name, it came out of my mouth as a moan. I felt his smile against my pink parts, and he said something, but it came out as vibrations where I was already wet. He took me to that desperate place quickly, the one where I feel the wall for places to hold on to, even though I know there's nothing. At last, I sank my fingers into his hair. I was a puller and a scratcher — two things Dylan liked about sleeping with me.

The sounds he made against me grew in intensity, as did the sense of impending freefall. "Dylan!" I tightened my grip and shouted his name as my body stiffened against his face.

He scooped me up and carried me the five steps it took to get to the bed, where he tossed me down and jumped on top. Air whooshed from my lungs, but I was too high from my climax to protest his rough handling. He slid into me, and I did not have time to wonder when he'd lost his pants.

"Oh, yes," he gritted out from between his clenched teeth. "You're still pulsing. I love the way you squeeze me. My Lacey." He planted a kiss on my temple, and that was it for the mushy stuff.

He wasn't gentle. He could be, when he wanted to. My Dylan could make the most tender love to me, give me the sweetest bliss in the world — or like now, he could take me fast and hard, letting his animal- istic side out to ride me into the sunset, or sunrise, as the case may be.

The pulsing of my orgasm grew more intense. He loved doing this to me, extending my climax until I couldn't stand it anymore. I lost my mind, writhing and arching under him, scratching at him so hard that he held my wrists down. He called my name, alternating it with the f-word, until he couldn't hold out any longer. His body surged forward, melding with mine as his climax throbbed in time with the party in my pussy.

He collapsed, rolling to the side so he wouldn't crush me. The irony of the situation always made me giggle. He didn't mind crushing me during the act, but afterward, he was all about treating me with loving care.

"I'm going to need another shower," I said as my wits and my breath returned. "And I guess it's officially a ponytail day."

He laughed and tried, unsuccessfully, to run his fingers through my hair. "I love the way sex hair looks on you."

I scooted to the edge of the bed. Sex hair made me look like a reject from an eighties music video. Dylan, on the other hand, rocked that fresh-from-bed, tussled look the way only an incredibly sexy man can. Fucker. Yep, that's jealousy talking. I knelt on the floor and lifted the dust ruffle so I could look under the bed.

"It's your fault, you know," he said.

I reached for his shoes, still in the shipping box. He'd ordered them online and had them shipped to my house, which, as I said, bothered me. The only thing he hadn't done was move his furniture from his storage unit. I've never lived with someone before, but I'm pretty sure a conversation usually happens before the actual moving. It should absolutely include the lines "We should move in together" and "Yes."

I handed the box to him. "What's my fault?"

"I'm a virile, twenty-five-year-old man. When I'm presented with the sight of a naked, beautiful woman, I just can't help myself."

He meant it as a compliment, but it struck me wrong—way too generalized. I chalked it up to my mood and growing discomfort with the way he'd taken our association from "just friends" to "cohabiting" in a matter of days. He'd come over after I'd broken up with Thomas, and he'd never left. My feelings for him were stronger than any I'd harbored for a man before, and the idea of not having him in my life gave me panic attacks, so I hadn't been exactly honest with him about how he was moving too quickly. While he was opening the brown box that contained his shoes, my expression turned as sour as my mood. Sex distracted me only for as long as it took to have it.

It was time for a quick rinse in the shower.

He came after me. Dylan didn't often let me alone when I was like this. "Thanks for finding my lucky shoes." His voice filtered through the shower curtain.

I didn't give a flying monkey about his shoes, but I kept that thought to myself. It was way too bitchy. "You're welcome." My voice sounded tight, and you'd think after just having a spectacular orgasm, I'd be surfing on the waves of a good mood.

"Lacey? Tell me what's stressing you out so much."

"Nothing," I said as I rinsed my hands. Yes, I was washing my hands in the shower. My OCD had to come out in some form, and this was it. However, from the day we met, Dylan had never been one to respect my bathroom privacy. "We need to get going. We're going to be late."

"We won't be late, not if you get out of the shower right now."

"I'm washing my hair." I wasn't. That was definitely a lie, but if he caught me washing my hands, he'd haul me out of there.

He opened the shower curtain and saw what I was doing. "Damn it, Lacey." He snagged the shower head from its cradle and hosed the sweat and smell of sex off me. While he was busy with that, I snuck in my sixth cycle of hand washing. "When we get home, we're going to sit down and have this out. You can yell, scream, and throw pillows at me, but you're going to tell me what's wrong."

I didn't want to. There was no nice way to tell him I didn't want him living with me. No matter how I rehearsed the speech, it always sounded like I was breaking up with him. I didn't want to do that, but I did want to slow down. I wanted to have rules and boundaries, and I knew it would hurt his feelings.

The idea of hurting him like that made me ache inside, an ache that brought guilt and all sorts of horrible baggage with it. Because no matter how much I wanted this relationship to work out, in the back of my mind, I kept thinking I didn't deserve him. Sure, he had some flaws, but he didn't lie to me, and he never hid my sunglasses. Besides, my OCD wasn't going away anytime soon. Maybe I didn't want to tell him to leave because I was afraid some time away would make him realize how truly fucked up I was and how unhealthy our relationship was. Perhaps he'd be better off without me, but I didn't want him to know that. And yet, if he didn't go, there was no way I could stop my OCD from getting worse.

He wrapped a fresh towel around me. "You have six minutes to get ready. I'll have breakfast and coffee ready to go. You can eat in the car."

Having a time limit of six minutes energized me, and I was ready to walk out the door at the appointed time. Dylan handed me a toasted English muffin stuffed with bacon and cream cheese.

I inhaled it before we made it to the car, at which point he finally handed over the coffee.

Once we were in the car, I got into full manager mode. I had a list of questions and topics the radio station had emailed me, and I used them to warm Dylan up. He wasn't an open book. Though his songs revealed things that were intimate and personal, he rarely talked about himself to anybody he didn't consider a close friend. Thank goodness the rest of the band would be meeting us there. Some of them were more willing to open up during an interview.

"What made you want to get into music?"

Dylan sipped his coffee, a stalling tactic that would work on television, but not on the radio. "My older sister plays percussion, and I idolized her growing up, so it was natural that I followed in her footsteps."

"Don't refer to Daisy as your older sister. She'll kill you."

He frowned.

"It's a girl thing."

"She's four years older than me."

"Yeah, and she's still young and hot, but you can't call her that either. Dylan, don't be difficult. Either refer to her as your sister or by her name."

He kept his eyes on the road. "Got it. How should I refer to you?"

That threw me for a loop. I recovered quickly. "You shouldn't refer to me at all. I'm not part of your band."

"I want to make sure you get credit for what you've done." He stuck his lower lip out in what he probably meant as a scowl, but it was too damned sexy to carry much weight.

"Your fans aren't interested in hearing about me. They want to hear from you and about you." Besides that, he knew how much I hated the spotlight. It made me wash my hands in an effort to refrain from telling terrible lies.

We got to the station on time, and the someone official was waiting in the lobby to greet us. Daisy, Levi, and Gavin were already there. Daisy hugged me, something she'd taken to doing every time she saw me. I wasn't sure if it had more to do with me being instrumental in launching their band toward the national stage, or if she was just happy to have Dylan out of her house.

Okay, so this is the part where I'm supposed to describe Daisy, Levi, and Gavin. It's been a few months since you've seen them, so

I'll do it. Daisy is the feminine version of Dylan. She has the same teal eyes and midnight hair. Last month, she got it cut almost as short as Dylan's, making their similarities even more pronounced. She's gorgeous and so very photogenic. I'm jealous of that quality. I might like the way I look in the mirror, but those qualities don't tend to translate into photographs.

Levi, god of the keyboard and violin (and violin-like instruments whose names I don't know), is tall, built, and handsome. He's a couple inches taller than Dylan and has a wiry frame. The first time I saw him without a shirt, I was surprised at the amount of muscles he has. He has brown hair and chocolate eyes that sparkle with excitement most of the time. He's also a champion worry-wart.

Gavin, who plays bass in such a way that he brings a haunting tone to Dylan's vocals, is about the same height as Levi. His blond hair falls past his ears, where it curls ever so slightly. He has enviable highlights that he comes by naturally. Like Levi, he has warm brown eyes. Both men are sweethearts.

Bryant Fullerton, the station manager of the Detroit area's only alternative radio station and the person there to greet us, held his hand out to Dylan. "Dylan Day, I'm Bryant Fullerton. I'm a big fan of your band. It's a pleasure to finally meet you."

"Same here," Dylan said. "I've listened to Eighty-nine X since I was a kid." He pulled me to the forefront of the group. "This is Lacey Hallem, our manager."

Bryant's mouth opened a little when he looked at me. He was average height for a man, with very broad shoulders and straw-straight blondish-white hair. I estimated his age somewhere north of thirty, but he could've been pushing fifty. I sincerely couldn't tell.

His gaze kept traveling downward, but he did a nice job keeping it mostly on my face. He took my hand, enveloping it in his for the handshake. It had the same amount of sincerity as the handshake he'd given Dylan, but his touch lingered a tad longer than necessary. His voice dropped lower when he spoke to me. "Ms. Hallem, it's a pleasure. The band will be in the booth, but you're welcome to listen and watch from the control room."

"Thanks. That sounds great." I lifted a bag I'd brought. It was full of shirts, stickers, and some autographed posters from the band's first photo shoot. "Here's some swag for your listeners."

Bryant took it from me. "Thanks." He steered me toward a door the receptionist had just buzzed open. "This way, please."

I glanced back over my shoulder to see Dylan scowling at the place where Bryant had his hand on my lower back. As politely as I could, I shrugged off his touch. While I don't want Dylan living with me, I also don't want to play stupid games with his affection. I caught Dylan's eye and gave him a reassuring smile. He relaxed a bit, but he was still on guard.

We were ushered down a hall and into separate rooms. Dylan gave me a long look before he followed Daisy through the door into the studio. His face was filled with displeasure and annoyance, and that set me off. What right did he have to be pissed at me? I could handle Bryant Fullerton, and I wasn't going to cling to Dylan's side like a simpering fool.

Once inside the control room, I took a deep, cleansing breath. This was not the time to run to the bathroom and wash my hands, and it was not the time to rub them together either. That often came across as wringing my hands, and it was counter to the image I needed to project.

Okay, so another thing you should know about today is that it was John's birthday. He would have been sixty. The only real father figure in my life had passed away from heart disease four months ago. Not a day went by that losing him didn't smack me somewhere soft and leave me struggling to deal with the pain. After this appearance, I guess Dylan and I were going to have it out about our living situation. But after that, I was going with my mother to visit John's grave. I hadn't said a word about any of this to Dylan.

In retrospect, I probably should have. What happened next might have been avoided if only I'd come clean about what was really bothering me. I think I was lying to myself by focusing on Dylan as the sole cause of everything going wrong with my emotions, though I couldn't deny the major role he'd played in throwing havoc into my life. Maybe. It's hard to tell, and I'm too fucked up to figure it out on my own.

I don't know. It's all so fucking confusing. I wish I had John to talk to. He would have helped me sort out the mess in my head.

Chapter Two

While I was watching Dylan, Daisy, Levi, and Gavin get situated in the studio, Bryant offered me the single free seat in the booth. Everything in there looked like it had a specific purpose, so I declined, and I was relieved when another person came in. The chubby young man had pasty skin and a black shirt that sported the station's logo. He looked like he spent all of his time indoors.

"This is Chuck," Bryant said. "He's the producer. The band will take calls, right?"

That was something we hadn't considered. I glanced through the window and contemplated my friends. Talking to fans was something they all loved, so I nodded. "They can take a couple. Do you screen them?"

"I will," Chuck said. "We'll look for someone who has an interesting question and can speak without giggling, pausing, or saying 'umm' fifty times a sentence."

As that description accurately described me when I'd met AFI during the brief time Kiss Me Goodnight had opened for them, I kept my mouth shut. In my experience, most fans are nervous, and even the glibbest talkers turn into blithering idiots when confronted with someone they admire.

I would have greeted Chuck with a handshake, but he sat in the single seat, ignored me, and started playing with the computer and controls. "It's nice to meet you, Chuck."

He lifted a hand in greeting but spoke into his headset, presumably to the DJ who would be interviewing the band. Through the glass separating us, I watched the foursome laugh and joke, but I couldn't hear what they were saying. It struck me that I was mostly here because I was Dylan's girlfriend. I mean, a band's manager doesn't follow them everywhere, do they? When they went on tour with AFI, I was only with them for three nights, and that was mostly because I missed Dylan.

Of course, that got me thinking about our living situation. Being such a private person, Dylan hadn't gone public with our relationship, and so I wondered why he was living with me when his status on all his social media still listed him as single. As far as anybody knew, I was merely his band's manager. Did that mean he wasn't sure about us?

"So, do you manage any other bands?" Bryant asked, derailing my journey down Anxiety Lane.

"No." I hadn't considered it. To take on another band, I would have to quit my job as a sales representative for Hanover Distribution. Then my supply of free liquor I didn't drink would dry up.

"Are you interested?"

When I looked up at him, he lifted his brow as if he'd just said the magic words to gain my undying devotion. I shrugged. "KMG keeps me busy."

The commercial break stopped, and the DJ introduced the band members. His first questions were simple, meant to put everybody at ease and establish an air of camaraderie. Then he (and I wish to hell I remembered his name) dove in and asked a question I knew would come up eventually, but I wished hadn't.

"Dylan, your songs contain some powerful lyrics. What inspires them?"

Dylan rubbed his jaw, probably in an effort to squelch a nervous laugh. As I said, outside of his songs, he isn't forthcoming with personal details.

Daisy laughed in that way only older sisters can. It filled me with a sense of dread, though Dylan seemed to be handling it better. "Mostly his girlfriend. We can always tell the state of their relationship by whatever new lyrics he brings us."

As he'd penned at least five songs currently in their rotation before he met me, I do not consider myself Dylan's muse.

The DJ's sidekick cackled. I'd heard him on the morning show before, and I hadn't liked him, so I knew he was going to say something crass. "So, if she was the one cheating on you in 'You Wish He Was Me,' is she also the one you were with when you screamed out the 'Wrong Name' in bed?"

When Dylan wrote "You Wish He Was Me," I hadn't connected it to me at all. We hadn't been dating, but the song was about Dylan's tortured thoughts while he'd been under the impression that I was sleeping with Thomas. I hadn't been — sleeping with Thomas, that is — so I still counted the song as a fantasy.

And "Wrong Name" still pissed me off. The first time I heard Dylan sing it, I punched him in the nose. He knows it's a sore spot, but it's their biggest hit right now, riding the air waves to the tops of various listener-powered request lists. There's no way they wouldn't play it or refrain from asking about it. The DJ spun the chorus of the song in question:

> *The devil in my head*
> *Invaded me in bed.*
> *It made me shout it out — I didn't want to shout —*
> *The wrong name.*

To his credit, Dylan winced. "The lyrics aren't a literal interpretation of actual events, and of course I took creative license with them. 'You Wish He Was Me' is about the angst present when you like someone but you haven't landed them yet."

The sidekick laughed. "Come on. How can 'Wrong Name' not be taken literally? I love that song. We've all done something like that before. I love the way you turn the tables and basically tell her to get over it."

In a nutshell, that's exactly what the song does, and that's why I hate it. Whenever it comes up in discussion, I feel humiliated anew. Waves washed over me.

Dylan cleared his throat. "It's a catchy song that lots of people relate to, and I would bet lots of other people have been on the receiving end of it and hate the song. I didn't intend for it to be so divisive. I'm thinking of putting an alternate version on the album, maybe change up the ending to a more conciliatory tone."

"No way, man," the DJ said. "It's great as-is. It's a single man's anthem for an 'oops' moment."

Only if that man wanted to stay single. The DJ looked like he was somebody's dad. I wondered if he was divorced, because no woman should have to put up with a man who doesn't value her as a person, and that's what "Wrong Name" meant to me.

"If he wasn't such a fucking manwhore, he wouldn't have that problem," I grumbled. I thought I'd said it quietly, but it had been clear enough for Bryant and Chuck to hear, and Chuck had turned on the microphone that led to the DJ's headset. Everybody heard.

"Manwhore?" The DJ smiled at me through the window. "Do tell."

Dylan also looked at me, a warning in his eyes that I tried so hard to not ignore. He even rubbed his hands together, telling me—for the first time ever—to go wash my hands. You know it's bad when he's actively trying to trigger my compulsion.

Invisible slime tickled over the skin on my hands, and I very much wanted to go wash them, but I resisted. I also resisted the lure of the DJ, which urged me to spin this into one of my best lies. I shook my head. As this was radio, they couldn't focus on me for long if I refused to talk, so that's what I did.

Unfortunately for us all, the DJ figured out that I was Dylan's girlfriend. Or maybe he'd done his research and knew who I was. While Dylan hadn't publicized our association, he also hadn't taken steps to hide or deny it. Or maybe the DJ was every bit the dickhead I thought he was. "So, Dylan Day, the object of your songs has just called you a manwhore. How do you respond to this prestigious accusation?"

Dylan's stoic glare was all the answer the DJ received. My accusation was wildly unfair. Dylan is the opposite of promiscuous.

Levi tried to save the interview. "That song might have been about a story I told Dylan after that happened to me. As you said, it's something that happens to a lot of people. We got to talking about it, and the next day, he had the lyrics ready to go to a song we'd already written."

I loved Levi. In that moment, I might have left Dylan for him. Dylan shot Levi a gratitude-filled look. He knows how badly this song affects me. They all know, even though it's one thing we never talk about. Dylan's offered to stop playing it several times, but I can't, in good conscience, ask them to take their first potential hit and hide it.

However, Levi's attempt at damage control didn't completely work, so Gavin jumped in with something witty, and Daisy changed the subject. Bryant tried to rein in his DJ by putting through a caller who gushed over the band and fixated on Dylan's physical attractiveness. She propositioned him, right there on the air, but this only gave the sidekick an opening to slide in a coughing "manwhore" reference.

It seemed I'd taught the morning show a new word, which they now took to using without impunity to refer to everyone and everything. They'd recorded me calling Dylan a manwhore, and by the next day, that sound bite was all over social media. As his manager, I regarded it as a nightmare. As the woman behind the lyrics, I felt a little vindicated. The person singing that song *seems* like a manwhore, at least.

I've said it before: Lying makes me feel better, and the fact that there tend to be no consequences for my actions only encourages me. However, in this crazy mess of a day, where there was surely going to be a full and flaming backlash to my lie, I finally felt like my life was in balance.

Of course, that balance was a fleeting illusion. I need to be reined in across the board. I need John to sit me down and sternly lecture me about my responsibility to be honest, especially with those I love and care about—but that isn't going to happen. The only person who has ever successfully taken me to task and made me want to be a better person has permanently exited my life. Still, part of me hoped maybe this mess would help me stop.

On the way home, Dylan fumed silently. I drove this time, as he tended to speed and cut people off when he was in a sour mood. When we were almost to my apartment, he said, "Aren't you going to apologize?"

I glanced at him, surprised he'd ask me to lie. "I'm sorry?"

"That's not going to cut it."

"I'm not sorry I said it," I said, wondering if that was actually true. "I'm sorry I hurt your feelings, but you know how I feel about that song." I turned into the parking lot and found the space designated for my apartment.

"You called me a manwhore, Lacey." His entire life, he'd slept with two women, one of whom had been his late wife. "That's not the image we're trying to project. We want fans to focus on our music, not our imagined bedroom antics."

I got out of the car. This was another "discussion" Dylan wanted to have. You know what I was spoiling for? An all-out fight. I had a lot of pent-up frustration and anger mixed with residual hurt and grief inside me, and that much emotion demands an outlet if I don't provide one.

On the plus side, the fact that I wanted to argue, scream, and yell boded well for the condition of my hands. Perhaps that's why Dylan listed those options earlier. He knew what I wanted before I did. I kind of resent him for that. People you're mad at aren't supposed to be right or accommodating. Dylan manages to be both. *Manwhore*.

He followed me into the apartment, hopefully noting the stiffness of my shoulders. I projected outrage as hard as I could. Lies to cover lies. I knew what I'd done was wrong, and it wasn't a little problem. I'd said it in front of the media. Not for the first time, I considered that I was a bad choice to manage his band. My mouth was bound to get negative press.

I went to the bedroom and into the closet. It's a large walk-in number half full of his clothes. I went to my dress section and began evaluating to figure out which one I would wear to John's grave. Though it had been chilly when we'd left this morning at an ungodly hour, the sun had come out for the return trip and warmed things up considerably. The ice in the parking lot was melting, and the early spring day promised to get even warmer. I selected a long-sleeved black velvet shirt and its matching full-length skirt.

Dylan stood in the doorway of the closet, deliberately blocking my path. He eyed the clothes in my hand incredulously. "What the hell are you doing?"

I responded with a neutral expression. "Changing."

This was my way of goading him. He has a temper, but it takes a lot to get him to explode. I have a hard time expressing anger, and I hate how Dylan gets eerily calm when he deals with me, so this is my way of compelling him to force me to let it out. Fucked up, right?

He took the clothes from me and threw them on the floor littered with shoes. Then he gripped my chin in his cupped hand, making me face him. "No. We're going to discuss whatever is eating you up."

I tried to shake my head, but he didn't let me move. "I'm fine."

"Liar. You're so *not* fine, it's not even funny. I haven't seen you this way in months."

If I took a step back, he'd let go of me and back off. I stared at him, wondering who was going to break first.

He studied me, searching my eyes for answers I didn't have. Why did I do and say things to drive him away when losing him was the worst thing I could imagine? Who the hell knew? Finally, he broke the silence. "You weren't calling me a name; you were lying."

"It's a fine line, isn't it?" I spoke softly and kept my gaze locked to his. "And at the end of the day, it doesn't actually matter."

"No," he agreed, releasing my chin. "It doesn't. The damage is done. You're going to have to deal with the fallout to make this right."

I wasn't prepared to handle public relations, but I nodded anyway. Tonight I was supposed to hang with Jane and Luma. I'd spill my tale of woe and ask for advice. Luma has a degree in public relations. She'd have some ideas.

He tried to take me in his arms, but I stiffened and pulled away. The whirligig of crappy emotions hadn't left the building. Dylan wasn't nearly as pissed as he should be.

He sighed. "You're a difficult woman to live with."

Oh, there it was—the opportunity my passive-aggressive side had been waiting for. I put my hands on my hips and squared up to him. "I never asked you to live here."

That's a bitchy thing to say, and I hadn't wanted to say it, but it burst out of my mouth like an alien baby. I envisioned all sorts of gross gooeyness spewing in all directions. From the look on Dylan's face, some of it definitely hit him.

He took a step back, turning away so I couldn't see his hurt. Now the door was no longer blocked, so I picked up my outfit and brushed it off. It's a good thing I don't have a pet cat who likes to hide out in the closet and leave fur everywhere.

I spread the skirt on the bed, checking for wrinkles that might need to be ironed. I know—somewhere a fashionista just cringed because I mentioned ironing velvet. Get over it.

Dylan sat down next to the clothes, putting himself near me but not in my way. "You never did, did you?"

There was no point in pretending I didn't know what he was talking about. I shook my head. "For months, all I got from you were these vague declarations and a few intensely passionate, drive-by kisses that neither of us really acknowledged. And then the day after John's funeral, you came over and never left. It's too much, too fast. I can't shift gears that quickly."

As I've said, this wasn't a discussion I was ever going to be prepared to have. I was terrified that he'd start listing reasons we shouldn't be together. Hot tears tracked down my face. I sniffled and tried to make them stop. Now that I'd started, I couldn't seem to stop talking either. Ignoring the *shut up, shut up* mantra playing through my head, I barreled on.

"I've never lived with somebody before. I've never even had to share space with a sibling. You've upended everything, and there are seventeen fucking pairs of shoes in the front hall. I can't take it. I can't deal with having you live here."

I hiccupped and choked, not adding in the counts I'd done of the different colors of his shirts that were not divisible by six. The need to wash my hands overwhelmed me, and I fled to the bathroom. Yes, it was crazy, but he'd known these things about me since the first time he'd followed me into a bathroom.

In another stunning turnabout, Dylan got there first and slammed the door closed before I could get inside.

I gaped at him. "Dylan, let me in there."

"No. I'm not going to let you run away. If you're going to break up with me, you're not taking a time-out to wash your hands in the middle of it."

More tears came, scalding my skin and my heart. This was what I'd been afraid would happen. "I'm not breaking up with you."

"You're asking me to move out?"

I nodded.

"Make fewer demands on your time?"

Again, I agreed. Living with somebody obligates you to share your comings and goings. It makes you accountable for your time, and I'm not ready for that. If I want to spend an hour wandering around the park looking at the spring foliage working its way through the snow and ice, it's nobody's business. Having to tell Dylan where I was going meant that either he'd want to come along, or he'd judge me for my actions, both of which horrified me. Some things I liked to do by myself. Perhaps if we'd been together longer, if we'd taken the time to know one another better, I would feel differently.

He ran his hand through his hair, though I noted he was careful to keep hold of the door knob so I couldn't duck past him. "It feels like a breakup, Lacey."

It shouldn't, because that's not at all what I wanted. "Dylan, I'm afraid that if we don't dial it back a few notches, it's going to lead to breaking up. Maybe I haven't done this before, but I don't think living with somebody should feel so stifling."

The teal of his eyes glowed ominously. "Stifling? Name one time I've stopped you from going someplace or hanging out with anybody. I don't require you to spend every moment with me."

"Damn it! I knew this wasn't going to turn out well. I hate talking to you sometimes." I whirled on my toe. I don't know how people whirl on their heels. I tried it once and fell over backward. The toe is a much easier balance point. Anyway, the bathroom wasn't the only place I could wash my hands.

Dylan tackled me as soon as I made it to the dining room. I'd gone about six steps before he figured out what I was doing. I landed on the floor with a thump that rattled stuff on the table and probably knocked some dust off my downstairs neighbor's light fixture.

Somehow, he'd managed to both push and catch me. My elbows were a bit sore, but the rest of me was fine. I lifted my ass in an attempt to dislodge him from my back. As he had more than sixty pounds on me, it didn't work.

"Answer my question, Lacey. Tell me how I stifle you!"

Given our current physical position, I found his demand rather funny. I laughed, and that wasn't easy to do with him squishing me against the floor. "Well, this is one way."

He turned me over and sat up, straddling my stomach. I knew he was only aiming to keep me from washing my hands, but I wanted to wash them. I needed to do it. I concentrated on my breathing, willing the compulsion to subside. Dylan was blissfully silent while I tamed one of my inner demons. I opened my eyes to find him watching me with a thin veneer of patience.

"Better?"

"Yeah. For now."

"I'm going to let you up, but if you head toward any place with running water, I will tie you to a chair until we're done talking."

I had to meet my mother in an hour. We didn't have all that long to talk. "Can't we do this later?"

He helped me to my feet. "Why? Do you have a hot date that just can't wait?"

I couldn't meet his gaze. I turned away and went into the living room where I flopped onto the sofa.

"Lacey?"

I heard the frown in his voice. I didn't need to see it on his face. I exhaled hard and closed my eyes. "It's John's birthday. My mom and I are going to put flowers on his grave."

The cushion sank as Dylan sat next to me. He took my hand in his. "Why didn't you tell me? I wouldn't have asked you to come this morning."

"I didn't want to tell you." I extracted my hand from his. "If you weren't living here, then I could come and go without having to answer all sorts of questions about my whereabouts. I'm not ready for this, Dylan. I don't want to tell you my every move, and I don't want you to think I need to know where you are every minute of the day."

"But you specifically wanted to keep this from me. Why?"

I flicked his jean-clad leg. "Stop analyzing me, counselor man. You know I hate when you do that."

"If I were analyzing you, I'd try to figure out the answer on my own and then lead you to discover the truth. I honestly don't know why you have a problem with any of this. I love you. You love me. This is where relationships eventually go. Living together doesn't mean I'm restricting your activities. It shows consideration to let the other person know where you're going and when you plan to be home."

This was like finding his fucking shoes. I thought I was being clear. Big neon lights should have been blazing around my key point — that our relationship had progressed too quickly for me to acclimate — but he didn't seem to see them.

"Dylan, when you met Nadia, you married her right away. You skipped the 'getting to know you' part of the relationship and went directly to the 'happily ever after' portion. Only you found out the hard way that it wasn't that simple. I don't want to move that fast. I want to take the time to get to know you, to let our relationship unfold naturally. I want us to last."

He sat forward and rested his elbows on his knees. His hands were clasped together, and I couldn't see his face. "You're saying you want me to back off and move out so we can build a strong foundation for our relationship?"

"We skipped the dating part, Dylan." Except for Thomas, every man I'd dated had skimped there. It was difficult to carry on a courtship when you had a wife waiting at home. Now that I was with a man who only had me in his life, I wanted more. "I want moonlight and roses."

Yes, I changed my mind about roses. In his hands, they would be romantic.

I knelt on the floor in front of him and touched the side of his face gently. "I want to try on a dozen outfits while I'm waiting for you to pick me up. I want to spend hours figuring out which lip gloss I should wear, even if I know I'm going to pick cherry because you love it so much. I want to be surprised by where you're taking me. I do *not* want to help you find your shoes."

He stared at me, a little dazed and lost. "For how long, Lacey? I like falling asleep next to you and waking up in the same bed. I like having a life together. I like when you complain about my shoes by the front door, and I like asking you to help me find stuff I've lost."

His pain constricted my heart, and the tears started anew. He brushed them away and pressed his forehead to mine. We stayed like that for several moments.

"Six weeks." I was comfortable giving him a timeline. "We can discuss it in six weeks. And then we can look for a larger apartment together. My place is really made for one person, or two people with far fewer clothes and shoes."

"Six weeks," he echoed. "I can give you six weeks. Now tell me the real reason you kept your plan to visit John's grave from me."

I didn't know how to answer that. I'd avoided thinking about it for so long, but now that he'd poked a hole in the dam of my silence, words came tumbling out so fast that I couldn't begin to snatch them back or organize them for coherence.

"John died and Thomas left and you moved in. It happened so fast, and I didn't know what to do with my feelings, so I've just been trying not to feel anything. I haven't grieved for him yet because I want to spend all day in bed just crying, but I know you won't let me. You'll drag me out and make me pretend to be happy when I'm dying inside, and I just want to let the pain out. And when I'm sad like that, I don't want you around. I don't want you to hug me or comfort me, and I don't want you sitting by my side when you could be doing dozens of other things."

He handed me a wad of tissues, which I balled up in my fists instead of using them to wipe away the sorrow ruining my makeup and turning my face into a blotchy mess that better matched what was happening on my insides.

I sprang to my feet and paced the room. It wasn't that large, so I didn't go far. "I keep lying to you. I did so well until he died, and then I started back up, and I can't seem to stop. Worse, I can't seem to want to stop. I know I should, but I like doing it, just like before I met you. It gives me such pleasure, and it makes everything feel better, if only for a little while. And I'm not sorry. I know I should be, but I'm not. I'm not. I did so well for so long, and now that's gone. I'm not the same person you fell in love with, Dylan. I'm the person I was before I met you, and I'm not sure you can handle that. If you ever choose to walk out of my life, I wouldn't blame you, not one bit."

Now I paused to wipe and blow. I got more tissue, and Dylan didn't stop me when I headed for the bathroom. I knew better than to wash my hands, but my face sure needed it.

Dylan came in after a few minutes. I knew he'd given me time to pull myself together, and I appreciated his thoughtfulness. He handed me a glass of water, which I drank.

"So, this is what I'm taking away from what you said: Moving too quickly with our relationship has interrupted your grieving process. You're unable to come to terms with the ways in which your life has changed, including my place in it, because I'm living here. You'd like me to move out, let you get your mental house in order, and then you'll discuss getting an apartment together. Is that accurate?"

I stared at him, shaking my head at his nonjudgmental tone. Damn, he was good with words. I fell a little more in love with him. "Why couldn't I have just said it like that?"

He put his arms around me, and I snuggled into his strong, comforting embrace. "Don't beat yourself up. You're good with words when you need to be. One of the ways I can tell you're being truthful is when your point takes some digging to find. I'm just relieved you're not breaking up with me."

"Being with me will never be easy." Even though I didn't want to, I felt compelled to issue a clear warning. "Maybe you should use the next six weeks to decide if you really want to mess with this kind of crazy."

He laughed. "I've already made my decision, Lace. I went into this fully informed, if not with a full understanding of what that information meant, and I'm not regretting a thing."

I tilted my face up, and he kissed me. I knew he wanted to make love to me, to assure me that his feelings hadn't changed, but I was pressed for time.

"Go get dressed," he said. "I'll call your mom and tell her you're going to be a little late."

Chapter Three

John was buried in a cemetery not far from my mother's house, where at one time we'd all lived together. He's near his family members who've passed on, and he purchased a couples plot, so my mother will someday rest beside him.

I know it's supposed to be a thoughtful thing, but it's difficult for me to not stare in horror at the empty place reserved for my mother. She's fifty-two. I want at least another fifty years with her, and that blank marble headstone mocks me with impending doom.

Mom held my hand. "Is there anything you want to say, sweetie?"

I had plenty to say, but now wasn't the time. "I miss him."

"So do I, baby. Talking helps. You know he's listening. He always listens."

I responded to my mom's prodding. John would want me to confide in him. If he could talk to me, he'd tell me to let it all out. Letting go of my mom's hand, I took a step forward. "John, I've fallen off the wagon. I can't seem to stop lying, especially to Dylan. Or about him. I asked him to move out so I could have some space to get my head together. He was very understanding, but I don't know how long that's going to last, especially if I keep going the way I have been."

Behind me, I knew my mom was chomping at the bit to say something, but she kept a tight rein on it. I appreciated her restraint.

"I don't know anymore why I do the things I do. I miss you so much. I don't think I can do this without you."

Mom put her hand on my shoulder. "Lacey, you can too do it. John told me you'd relapse a few times before you fully acclimated to a lie-free lifestyle. He said you'd fall hard, and you were going to need us to help you. He's gone, but I'm here. I'm always here for you."

I turned around and let my mother fold me into her soothing embrace. There were no demands waiting just below the surface. She wanted nothing but for me to be happy. "I love you, Mom. I didn't want to relapse. I hate hurting Dylan, but I can't seem to stop."

She smoothed her hand down my back. "I know, baby. Let's go home. I'll make some tea, and we'll make German chocolate cake to celebrate John's birthday, and you can tell me all the details. I've been looking forward to giving you relationship advice since you were a teenager."

I looked up at my mother, taking in the way her beautiful auburn curls billowed around her pretty face. Her brown eyes shone with tears, and I realized I was in for an earful. She was definitely going to tell me things I needed to hear, and she'd try her best to fill in for John.

"Can I take a slice back for Dylan? He loves German chocolate."

"Of course you can." She took my hand again. "We'll put aside half of it. Dylan has a healthy appetite."

Once we made it to her house, Mom got down to business. Over the past few months, she'd unearthed all of her favorite cookbooks. She'd kept the healthy ones she'd bought when John started having problems with his heart, but she'd added her old ones back to the shelf. They had some very good recipes, and while Genevieve Zimmerman didn't see a reason to cut back on healthy eating, she now applied what she'd learned from that to some of her older recipes, reducing the fat content and upping the healthy factor in some of her preferred dishes.

"Okay, sweetie. Let's start with you telling me why having a close and intimate relationship with a man freaks you out."

That's a question John would have asked. I sighed. "I'm not having flashbacks to my father, if that's what you're thinking." John and my mom had provided an excellent example of how two people could have a successful, loving relationship. A thousand-watt bulb lit my brain. "How long had you and John been dating before he moved in with us?"

Mom sifted flour into her mixing bowl. She bit her lip as she thought. "About six months? That would have been a year after we'd met. But honey, we had to be careful. He was your therapist, and neither of us wanted to set back the progress you'd made."

I don't recall making much progress until after John moved in with us and I stopped seeing him professionally. It was like he rolled all his therapeutic strategies into being the best dad in the world to me, and that worked miracles.

In six weeks, it would be very close to the one-year anniversary of when I'd met Dylan. I took tremendous comfort in that association.

"How long did it take for us to adjust to having him here?"

She shrugged and moved aside to let me start folding in the wet ingredients. "I don't remember. I think we all made little adjustments every day, and then, after a while, it was normal. I think the key is remembering to be patient, because nobody is going to live in a space the same way you do. It's unrealistic to expect not to make sacrifices and change the way you do things."

For me, changing too many routines at once has a ripple effect on my entire day. I think I'd been tolerating Dylan's presence, treating him like a visitor to my home, and he'd overstayed his welcome. I wanted so badly to have him in my life, but this wasn't how I wanted it to happen. "I told Dylan we could talk about moving in together in six weeks. I said we could look for a new place. I think it'll be easier for me to adjust if everything is new."

"Perhaps," Mom said. She took the mixing bowl and poured the contents into two round pans. "If nothing else, six weeks will give you some time to put it into perspective and be ready to discuss how you want things to be. I'm sure Dylan wasn't completely happy with the arrangement either. When you don't want someone in your space, you can be quite unfriendly."

That's a kind description. It's probably similar to one Dylan would've used. Sometimes I don't understand why he loves me, but I know without a doubt that he does.

When I got home later that afternoon, Dylan wasn't there. Little things struck me at first. His pile of shoes was missing from the front hall. The stacks of sheet music that had been on the table and counter were gone. His eReader wasn't charging on the TV stand. The boxes of cereal he never put away—I didn't eat cereal, so they were all his—weren't on top of the refrigerator anymore. In the bathroom, his razor and shampoo were absent. And in the bedroom, his clothes no longer took up half the closet.

I sat on the bed, too stunned by the reality of the situation to cry. He'd left. I'd asked him to move out, and all traces of him had vanished from my life. Now I felt rejection and desolation, two things I had no business feeling. This was my fault. He'd only done what I'd wanted.

I knew where he was and what he was doing. He had practice at Daisy's house—his house once again. But now that he was gone, and we didn't have plans, I could only think of the way he'd treated me before we decided to be together: vague declarations, hot kisses, and no follow up. Is that what I'd asked for?

Before I could work myself into full panic mode, my cell phone rang. It was Dylan. I pressed the button to accept the call. "Hi."

"Hey, Lace. Are you home yet?" He sounded out of breath.

"Yeah."

"Are you okay?"

"Yeah."

"Are you lying?"

"A little."

He didn't say anything, but I could hear him processing my lie in the silence on the other end. "How's your mom doing?"

I looked at my lap, and for the first time, I noticed I was still holding the container filled with cake. "We made cake. I brought some home for you."

He chuckled uneasily. "You're having dinner with Jane and Luma tonight."

"Yeah." We almost always stay out late.

"I thought we could go out tomorrow. You know, like on a proper date."

I perked up. "Really? Where?"

This time, his chuckle had a lot more confidence in it. "Spoilers, Lacey. It's a surprise. Wear something pretty. Afterward, you can invite me back to your place for some cake." He put special emphasis on the last word, giving it a spicier meaning.

I laughed. "Okay," I giggled. Tension drained away, and the prospect of sleeping alone tonight seemed a lot less foreboding. I needed space, and Dylan was giving it to me. "What time?"

"Six, of course. Listen, I have to go. We're working through a newer song, and when we go into the studio next week, we want to have everything perfect. I love you."

"I love you too."

Jane chose the venues that night. She took us to a place that served killer barbeque, and then she took us to a bar that had live music. Since stumbling upon Kiss Me Goodnight, I hadn't spent much time listening to other local acts. But once upon a time, the three of us had regularly spent our evenings checking out whatever was new. If we liked a band, we would see them a couple of different times. But most bands we liked came and went within six months, so some we only managed to catch once before they imploded.

The bar had a decent crowd. I think most of them, like me, were surprised to see live music on the bill for a Monday night. That seemed more like a weekend thing.

Jane and Luma exchanged a look as we sat down at a table near the stage. We each ordered something to drink. I was the designated driver—I was afraid I'd start crying if I got drunk—so I was surprised when they both ordered nonalcoholic beverages as well.

"All right," I said. "What gives? Did Dylan call you?"

Luma shook her head. "Why would Dylan call me?" Her eyes grew suddenly wider. "Lacey, did you guys get into a fight? I saw on Twitter that you called him a manwhore on the radio. I thought it was funny, but I can see where he wouldn't."

Heat crept up my face at a record rate. I fanned myself. "Shit. Twitter?"

Jane laughed, probably at how red I was. "Check hashtag manwhore."

I whipped out my phone and saw that the damage was worse that I'd expected, and it sure wasn't local. Everybody had jumped on that party bus. On the positive side, the number of followers for @KissMeGoodnight had grown by nearly ten percent. "Dylan's going to kill me."

I checked their other social media, and then I checked the sales of their singles. "Wrong Name" had sold almost two hundred copies today alone, and "Kiss Me Goodnight," the only other song the record company let us keep up there for downloading, had sold over a hundred. I texted Dylan the good news.

Hey—huge sales today.

Stop working. And have fun with J and L, he responded after a moment.

Okay, so yes, my comment ended up being good for growing their fan base, if not exactly the way Dylan wanted it done. But there were other repercussions. A few minutes later, Daisy texted me. *Manwhore is embarrassed. He's been getting some seriously fucked-up sexual offers.*

I didn't know how to respond to that. I texted Dylan. *Sorry. I didn't mean to put you out there like that.*

Gavin texted me next. *Can you call me manwhore next time?*

Levi joined the fun. *Ignore G. I'm next. I wanna have my balls sucked by identical twins.*

Dylan got back to me. *I'm over it. I love you. Have fun OK? Text me when you get home so I know you're safe.*

I spent the next ten minutes compressing my sins into a short tale and answering Jane's and Luma's questions about my behavior. Having talked about it already with my mother, I didn't feel the need to seek more counsel. Rather, I shared the insights I'd gained from my earlier conversation.

"That sounds reasonable," Luma said. "I'm looking forward to you getting back on an even keel. You act like lying doesn't bother you, but it does. You think it makes you feel better, but it doesn't. You use it to push people away, and when they go, it's proof you weren't worth it in the first place."

"It's a vicious cycle," Jane added. She crunched an ice cube in her mouth as she spoke. "Like my former infatuation with Owen. I finish my internship next month, and I already have a job offer. I've stopped selling myself short. Now it's your turn."

Luma and I both made the obligatory disgusted faces when Jane mentioned Owen. Though Jane had nursed a crush on him through much of law school, he hadn't returned her feelings. Instead, he'd used her as a free tutor to help him squeak by. In the process, he'd run all over her feelings and her self-esteem. He was a jerk, and I was glad to see her finally getting over him.

"Good for you," I said. Dismissing the part where Luma and Jane had analyzed me, I lifted my drink. "Here's to breaking vicious cycles."

They joined in the toast, and we all drank.

"So, Lacey, Jane and I really like the band that's going to perform tonight. We have a proposition for you." Luma regarded me with expectant eyebrows lifted halfway to her hairline. It was a comical look.

"Okay." I heaved a resigned sigh. "But we have to take pictures. I promised Dylan that if I ever got frisky with a woman, he'd get to see it."

Luma's expression didn't change until Jane laughed, and only then did she seem to get the joke. She rolled her eyes. "You're not my type."

I pretended to pout. "Bitch."

She shrugged. "Maybe after a few drinks. Ask again later. Seriously, though, we set this up for you."

I stared at her. "Set what up?"

The band came onstage. It consisted of four women. Each was dressed in the goth vein, and by that, I mean they were layered in black. The lead singer had fire-engine-red hair. It gave the quartet a little color. The two guitarists were blondes, and the drummer's hair matched her clothes. We were close enough to see their generous black eye makeup—the raccoon look. Two wore red lipstick, and the lead singer and drummer had opted for black.

"Good evening, Detroit! Are you ready for Something Wicked?"

From the way she said it, I figured Something Wicked was the name of the band. I wondered if they were alluding to Shakespeare or Ray Bradbury. Either way, it was a good name.

Jane gestured to the stage. "It's time we started a talent management company. I'll be the legal expert, and Luma will handle public relations. In my internship, I focused on contract law. Tonight, we've arranged with the owner of this place to let Something Wicked perform for us. They're going to do a five-song set."

And then they wanted me to sign up to manage the band? Daisy, Levi, Gavin, and Dylan practically had to twist my arm, and even then I'd only taken it because we were friends. I was not sold on this idea, but Something Wicked started playing, and we were too close to the speakers for meaningful conversation. Goth music wasn't currently marketable, so I didn't hold out much hope for this quartet. Even if I liked their sound, that didn't mean they'd sell songs.

As they played, I thought about the idea of forming our own company. We could call it LLJ. My name would go first because I was already in the business. I began forming a business plan in my head, and I tuned out the band while I daydreamed about being my own boss.

"Lacey!" Jane hissed, pulling me from a wondrous fantasy.

I blinked. "What?"

"Listen to the music."

"I *am* listening." Lie—one of my more innocuous attempts.

"Are not. You said something about working in your pajamas."

"Oh." That was the dream: making money while not having to wear real clothes. And also not be a hooker.

Part of me had judged them by their costumes and dismissed them out of hand. I had to clear that from my mind and actually listen. If I hadn't done that the first time I'd seen Dylan's band, I might have just stared at the beef onstage and not really heard their sound. Looking at Something Wicked distracted me, so I closed my eyes.

They were surprisingly good, though not as good as KMG had been the first time I heard them. Something Wicked had a sound that blended influences like Paramore, No Doubt, and Yeah Yeah Yeahs. They needed something a little more distinctive if they didn't want to be lumped in with the rest of the lookalike, sound-alike girl rockers, but at least they didn't sound dark and depressing. Though I liked the goth sound, I didn't need to hear that kind of music right now. Then, just when I was about to write them off as contrived and amateurish, they threw in a slow song. In this genre, the lead singer showed her true talent. She had a gorgeous voice, the kind that demanded attention—when she used it effectively.

I went into full analytic mode. Had their music detracted from the best instrument in their band? The next song addressed my concern. It had a section where the music faded to highlight the vocals, and that really made the song pop. They finished their set and thanked the audience. I liked a band with manners.

Turning to my potential business partners, I said, "If they can write more songs like those last two, I think they have a fighting chance. If not, they're doomed to be a local act until they disband and give up."

Luma considered this. "I think their other songs are good. You weren't really listening."

Kiss Me Goodnight had some songs they'd rotated out of their repertoire once they'd written better music. Luma was right about me not listening to all of the songs, but I wasn't going to cede the point. "Not good enough. A song should draw me in, make me want to listen to it. The last two did that. The first three did not."

"So, what do we want to tell them?" Jane said. "They know they're auditioning for the person managing Kiss Me Goodnight."

I pursed my lips. "You used KMG's name to lure talent to our company?"

Luma giggled. "Yep. Do I know marketing or what?"

Honestly, I had no idea. Since graduating from college almost a year ago, Luma hadn't worked a day in the field. "Okay, Jane. What kind of paperwork do we have to fill out to form a company? I know the government is going to be all up in our business from the get-go."

"Absolutely," Jane agreed. She extracted a folder from her large purse. Now I knew why she was lugging that behemoth around. We usually only took it to the movies so we could smuggle in water bottles (or liquor) and snacks. The one time they'd asked to search it happened to be the one time it'd been full of adult diapers and tissue. (The adult diapers hadn't been for Jane. She'd come from her great-grandmother's house, and her nana had filled her purse. Jane argued that the woman was senile, but I didn't agree. I thought she had a wicked sense of humor. At any rate, the manager at the theater had turned ten shades of red and stammered an apology.) "I have the forms filled out. Luma and I signed already."

I motioned for the file. Forming a company with my best friends was probably the best career move I could make. What else could a lawyer, a marketing major, and a finance/business admin major do? This was *destiny*. Even as the word popped into my head, I deleted it. The idea of preordained stuff still rubbed me wrong. We'd chosen our careers based on our interests. It wasn't fate; it was the logical outcome of our life experiences. Yeah, it was impulsive, but you know I roll that way.

The name of the company had been filled in. Instead of going with simply LLJ, they'd called it LJL Talent. I could live with that, and it meant LL Cool J wouldn't be suing us for using something close to his name. Letting myself imagine meeting him in person (shirtless) for a moment—lawsuit or not, that man was seriously hot—I probably got a dreamy expression on my face. My friends could think I was happy about forming a company. It wouldn't be untrue, just not the source of my smile.

After signing, I handed the papers back to Jane.

"I'll file these. Once I get a TIN, you'll need to open up accounts in the name of the business." She paged through everything to make sure it was in order. "Luma, get going on a logo. Now, Lacey, let's talk about Something Wicked."

I shook my head, and not because I had no clue what "TIN" meant. "I don't like their look, and I only liked two songs. I need to hear more and get to know them before I make any kind of decision." I had to fall in love with them the way I'd fallen for KMG.

Luma heaved a fake long-suffering sigh. "I told you, Jane. Lacey isn't going to make a snap decision. Look at how long she knew KMG before she decided to manage them." She grinned to let me know she was on board with taking this a little slower.

"But they're so good," Jane said. "I want to do for them what Lacey did for Kiss Me Goodnight."

I had no desire to invest that kind of time and energy in a band I wasn't sure about. "Jane, I put a lot of hours into KMG. It's more than making a few phone calls and attending a meeting or two with the band. It's emails and swag, repeated calls to venues, station managers, suppliers. Then there's all the other stuff—dealing with contracts and payment and publicity. It's not a small job."

Luma put her hand over mine. "But there are three of us to handle it now. It's not you doing this alone. You've blazed all the trails. I know it won't be easy moving forward, but it won't be as difficult as it's been going it alone."

She had a point there. I'd established relationships with some key people in key places, and KMG was becoming more popular by the day. I relented. "I still want to see them again."

Jane tilted her head. "Here they come. I asked them to join us after their set." She stood for the gruesome foursome coming at us. Jane greeted them with handshakes and hugs, and then she introduced them. "This is India Kingston, the lead singer. Bree Martin plays keyboard. Charlotte Christie plays lead guitar, and Violet Piper is on drums."

I shook hands with each of them, as did Luma. It made sense that they'd met Jane and Luma before, but I made a mental note to ask Jane how she first encountered the band. "It's nice to meet you. Pull up chairs."

They did, and we crammed seven around a table meant for four. It worked out okay.

"Well," India ventured. She looked uncertain under all that heavy makeup. "What did you think?"

I gave her a brutally honest answer. Once she got to know me, she would appreciate the fact that I hadn't lied to her. "The last two songs were good, but I didn't care for the first three. Your voice is your band's best instrument. You need arrangements that highlight it more. Also, the way you dress isn't going to win you the fans you'll need to be successful. Your music and your act isn't theatrical enough to be the next version of Kiss or ICP."

Bree turned up her nose at me. "This is our style."

I'd done a tour of duty through the goth scene as a teen. I had a healthy appreciation for the style of dress and the music, but let's face it: no true goth band has ever been wildly successful. At the most, they get just a fringe following (and, really, their die-hard fans are happy about that). I wasn't against a fringe following — that's what KMG had right now — but even that level of success wasn't guaranteed.

"It's fine to want to identify with a subculture, but you need to add something of your own to the mix. This is the uniform of a million disaffected teens or wanna-bes. Your look needs to appeal to a wider audience. I want to see a practice session, and I want to see how you look on a normal day." I had a hunch their casual style would suit the stage just fine.

Violet, the drummer with the all-black thing going on — including hair and lipstick, said, "You're evaluating us on our style? I've seen Kiss Me Goodnight. They usually wear black T-shirts and jeans."

They do, but they also dress that way normally. It isn't a costume as much as an attempt to have coherence on the stage. "And they look great. Nothing detracts from the visual and auditory experience of the audience. You get eye candy and sweet sounds."

Violet sighed and closed her eyes, revealing entirely too much black eye shadow. "Gavin Reid is so cute."

Charlotte, the heretofore silent guitarist, shook her head. "Levi is way hotter."

India rolled her eyes. "Everybody looks at Dylan Day. He's handsome, built, and that man can sing. I'd love to do a duet with him."

I didn't get the sense that was a double entendre, but I ignored it anyway. The idea of working with anybody in another band right now wouldn't fly with him. He was focused on cutting KMG's first studio album, and that's where I wanted his attention to remain.

"Getting back to Something Wicked," Jane said. She looked at me nervously. Perhaps India had mentioned finding Dylan attractive before, and Jane wanted to avoid the topic. It didn't bother me. The more popular the band became, the more women (and men) threw themselves at the various band members. Audra, Daisy's life partner, and I had discussed the phenomenon a few weeks ago, and we'd agreed that the Day siblings didn't suffer from wandering eyes or hands. Dylan often didn't notice when somebody was flirting with him, and when he did, he was usually embarrassed.

"Yeah," Luma chimed in. "Call Jane and let her know when your next three practices are."

"So, you like us?" Bree asked. She stared at me expectantly, as if I had the final say. I guess I did. Jane and Luma already liked them.

"We'll see," I said. "No promises."

I wasn't aiming to be a dick, but I didn't want them to think I was over the moon about them when I wasn't. I like to think I have good taste and good instincts.

The ladies made themselves scarce, and Luma turned to me. "I picked this next band."

My jaw dropped. "How many are we seeing tonight? This was supposed to be fun, not business."

Jane lifted her virgin daiquiri in a toast. "We get to write off this entire night."

"Just one more," Luma said. "We each picked one we thought had potential."

Five guys came on the stage. I immediately liked their style a lot more than Something Wicked's. They each wore a dress shirt, jeans, and boots. One of them had flip flops on, which I found interesting. Their movements were tentative and nervous. They kept stealing glances at us as they tuned their equipment. This performance was going to suck if they didn't settle down. I decided to take matters into my well-washed hands.

I went up to the stage and waved the nearest band member over. "Hi. I'm Lacey."

He hopped down and shook my hand. Now that we were on the same level, I could see that he was several inches taller than Dylan. His brown eyes sparkled with energy and excitement. "Leonidas, but you can call me Leo. I play bass." He motioned the others to us.

"This is Ari, our singer. Max plays lead. Bennett is the beatkeeper. Bastien plays keyboard, piano, violin, cello—and about ten other instruments. I play violin and cello too."

I shook hands with them all. Leo was much better looking than Ari, but that arrangement had worked out well for Fall Out Boy. The one in the flip flops turned out to be Bennett. "What are you guys called?"

Bennett puffed up and stepped forward with a huge, suggestive grin on his face. "Latin Cousin."

I took a closer look at Bennett, the way you do when some guy you hadn't considered *that way* got into your female space and made you give him a brief once-over. Most likely, I appeared baffled. Since Dylan and I had been together, I hadn't shopped around. Bennett had sandy brown hair, a strong jaw, and a round face with friendly features. He wasn't bad looking, but he was several years younger than me. I wasn't sure it was legal for him to be in this bar.

"Latin Cousin?" I tried to reserve judgment. I didn't like their name, but I didn't want to come right out and say that before their performance. My goal was to set them at ease so I could hear their best work.

"Yeah." Bennett leaned even closer. His aftershave smelled good, but his attempt at flirting made me want to laugh. "You know what they say about Latin cousins?"

I didn't, and I wasn't sure I wanted to. With one finger, I pushed his chest, directing him to give me space, which he did. He definitely amused me, but Dylan wouldn't find his over-the-top flirting funny. "You sure have a lot of swagger."

Bennett's grin grew. "You look familiar. I think we might have met in a past life."

That had to be one of the worst pickup lines I've heard. Before I could give him the brush off, Bastien tugged at Bennett's arm. "Let's jump onstage and show her we're more than swagger."

They had a unique sound that reminded me of a cross between OneRepublic, the Black-Eyed Peas, and Phoenix. I liked them, though they clearly needed more practice. In two of the songs, they were playing at different speeds. It's never a good thing when the singer is behind the beat or when the guitarist and the drummer clash.

Luma gave me a superior smile. "I suppose you want to see them practice too?"

"Yeah." I didn't want to sign bands just because we'd formed a company. "I can't represent a band I don't believe in, and I can't believe in anybody I don't know."

The boys strutted over to us afterward. Leo parked himself on one side of me, and Ari took his position on the other. I guessed they were shielding me from Bennett's forward passes.

Ari greeted us and repeated the introductions. "Well? What did you think?"

I wasn't as impressed as they wanted me to be. Luma answered. "Email me the times and locations of your next three practices. We want to drop in and see how you work."

Max frowned. "Isn't that what you told the girls?"

Peering closer, I realized Max looked a lot like Charlotte. "You guys are friends with them?"

"Charlotte is Max's twin," Leo answered. "We all grew up together, and we share a practice space."

That might prove awkward if we decided we liked one more than the other. I tried to handle this diplomatically. I took a sip of my drink and riffled through my head for the best way to phrase my misgivings. "I don't like the name of your band."

You know how lies have a way of bursting out of my mouth? It seems the unvarnished truth found the same pathway.

Chapter Four

The next day, I experienced fly-by creepy-crawly sensations in my stomach. It took me some time to remember what nervous anticipation felt like. The last person I'd dated was Thomas, and even though his dates usually involved a plane ride, I don't recall ever feeling this excited.

This was my first official date with Dylan, and I did everything I ever dreamed of doing in preparation. By the time I'd settled on a forest green tunic (that I felt would bring out the teal of his eyes) and dark cream leggings, my bedroom looked like a tornado had hit it. I liked wearing tunics. This one was tight around my breasts and cut low enough to keep a man's interest, especially if said man was a breast man, which Dylan was. It fell around my hips in a way that accented my assets nicely. I admired myself in the full-length mirror hanging on the back of my closet door, wondering which parts Dylan would like the best. The buzzer on the door sounded while I was cleaning up my mess.

I hopped down the stairs to answer it, blissfully aware that I was going to make us late. My makeup needed fixing, and I hadn't done a thing to my hair. I wanted to wear it up. Right now it was having a bit of a wild time. Changing clothes so much had definitely fluffed my curls.

Dylan smiled when I opened the security door, and the look of appreciation in his eyes grew as he looked me up and down. As I'd predicted, his gaze lingered the longest at chest level.

He'd dressed up too. Gone was his normal T-shirt-and-jeans uniform. He wore a black button-down shirt and gray slacks. The first few buttons on the shirt were undone. On his feet, he wore his lucky shoes. The TARDIS blue was the only real color on him.

I gave him a low, appreciative whistle. It may or may not have been offensive. I suspected I was still on thin ice after calling him a manwhore. "Come on in, handsome. I'm not quite ready to go."

He laughed, clearly not offended. "That's okay. I'm early. I was going to wait in the car for another half hour, but I missed you too much."

I got up on my tiptoes and threw my arms around him. He obliged by kissing me senseless. The security door slammed, and when he set me down, I realized he'd picked me up and brought us both inside.

"I missed you too," I said. "Not having you here is different than I thought it would be."

He lifted a brow and put his hand on the small of my back, guiding me up the stairs to my apartment. "Good different or bad different?"

I hadn't expected a question. I thought he might commiserate or offer to move back in, not ask for a value judgment I hadn't made. "I don't know. I guess I thought it would be just like it was before, but it's not."

"Nothing ever is."

We'd made it to my apartment, but he didn't reach for the door. In all ways, he was showing me this was my space, that he respected my need for clear boundaries and transitions. I opened the door and motioned him inside. "I won't be long. Make yourself at home."

The rest of my preparations were quick — Dylan wasn't a fan of a lot of makeup on a woman. I made sure to put on cherry lip gloss, and I slipped the tube into my purse. He'd disposed of several of my other glosses. My man was not fan of orange or strawberry. He liked the fruits just fine, but not as flavoring for my lips.

He knocked on the door just as I finished pinning my hair in place. I opened it, and he pushed his way into the room. In short order, I found myself against the wall. Dylan wrapped his arms around me and captured my lips. The onslaught didn't last long, but it left me breathless.

"Did you think I was washing my hands?"

Mentioning them meant he was going to have a look. It was human nature. I let him. For once, they weren't so bad. The redness had mostly faded. "You haven't been washing them."

"Only at appropriate times," I assured him. "I'm trying, Dylan. With everything."

He picked at the hair near my temple, drawing down a curl. "I appreciate that, Lacey. I know it's hard, but you can do this. You're stronger than you think."

We held the moment for several seconds, and then I had to look into the mirror so I could fix my hair. I was certain we both planned for the night to have a happy ending, so I knew my hair would end up as disheveled as he liked, but that didn't mean I wanted to go out looking that way.

"Leave it," he said. "I like seeing your curls. It's sexy."

Since he hadn't pulled out more than a few locks, I let it go.

He took me to an upscale restaurant that served Asian cuisine. I liked spicy, so I stuck with Chinese. Hunan was my favorite. He went for a mild Korean dish. When the food arrived, I dove in.

Dylan watched me, an amused sparkle in his eyes. "Careful. Remember what happened the last time you had Hunan."

The spiciness wasn't immediately apparent, which is how I liked it. The initial bite went down smoothly, and it wasn't until after you'd enjoyed the other flavors that the heat snuck up on you. I liked wily foods. But I did take his warning into account, and I waited for it to hit me. It did not.

"How's your food?"

He shrugged. "Not much flavor to it. I don't understand why the fried rice has peas and corn in it, and there's no soy sauce."

I also had expected Asian vegetables. I liked pea pods and water chestnuts, broccoli, bamboo, and mushrooms. The place on the corner where I got takeout also included spicy black beans. It was to die for. This was the sanitized version.

"It's not spicy," I said. "It tastes like fried chicken and rice." The sauce had more in common with barbeque than any Hunan I'd tasted.

He reached across the table and took my hand in his. "Tell me about your day."

My day hadn't been remarkable. "I sold liquor. Last night was better. Jane, Luma, and I formed a company — LJL Talent Management. We're scoping out local acts to represent."

Dylan's eyebrows lifted, and a wry smile accompanied the look. "We had to beg you to represent us."

"I know," I said. "But it turns out I'm not bad at it. Jane will handle the legal aspects, which is good because I have to pay a lawyer to look over all the contracts as it is. And Luma is going to handle marketing and publicity, which I suck at."

"You don't suck at it." Dylan sipped his cola. He hadn't let go of my hand yet, and I didn't want him to. "You just don't enjoy it the way you do other aspects of managing a band. You're good at giving advice and feedback, coming up with a plan — things like that."

This was true. I was good at figuring out what needed to be done, and it would take a great deal of stress away from me to have other people carrying out the plan.

"I'm happy for you, Lacey. As your company takes off, you might find you'll have to quit working for Hanover. You won't have time to do both. Right now, you devote a lot of time to Kiss Me Goodnight. And I know you too well to think you'd half-ass the job for anyone you represent. You might be a bit volatile and unpredictable, but when you give your word, you don't go back on it."

Warm fuzzies made me forget the lackluster food. His blessing meant a lot. Except for my mom and John, nobody's opinion had ever mattered that much to me. As much as I loved Jane and Luma, their disapproval of what I wanted had never stopped me from going after it. I refer here to the relationship mistakes I've made in the past. While I did enjoy their sanctioning of my relationship with Dylan, if they'd hated him, I would still have dated him.

"You believe in me that much?" I think I blushed. Either that, or hot flashes were coming on thirty years before I expected them.

"You can do anything, Lace. Anything at all. You're good at managing us. You enjoy it, and we're thankful for everything you've done. If this is what you want to do, I'm going to support you."

I basked in everything he gave me, and I finally understood why he'd been so in awe of the way I'd supported and encouraged his dream. Perhaps I hadn't known what my dream was, but now that I did, I embraced it with my whole heart. It made a difference to have Dylan in my corner; it seemed anything I wanted to achieve was just a matter of hard work and time.

After dinner, he took me to a park. A small river meandered through it. We walked alongside the gently flowing water, holding gloved hands as we navigated the packed-dirt path. As befitting the first week of spring, we wore warm winter coats. The snow had melted, but the air was frigid. This kind of date would totally rock once the temperature made it north of fifty.

"I'm sorry I called you a manwhore."

He shook his head at the word. "Thanks for the apology. I'm not mad at you. I think I was more shocked that you would say something so uncomplimentary about me."

I'd said worse about people I had no right to malign. I'm not saying I had a right to malign Dylan, just that we had enough baggage between us to warrant some hostility. He left off the part where I'd hurt his feelings, so I guessed he really was over it.

"I want to stop," I said. It was true. I didn't know if I could, but the desire was there, and that was new. "When life was getting overwhelming, John used to help me out. I know he wasn't my official therapist—at least not for long—but he functioned as something even better. I miss having him to talk to."

Dylan squeezed my hand. "Are you going to start seeing somebody?"

I couldn't imagine talking to a stranger about my life. It had taken a series of horrible events for me to confide in Dylan. "I've started talking to my mom. She's very understanding. I think I was reluctant to talk to her before because whenever I used to have a hard time, I could see how much it hurt her. I didn't want to cause her more pain, so I turned to John. He was very good at separating his feelings from our discussions so I could tell him whatever was on my mind."

We came to a stopping point. Ahead, a strip mall cut off the tree-lined paths and playground. As one unit, we turned around.

"I can't do that for you," Dylan said. "I'd like to say I can, but it's damned hard to separate my feelings from our discussions. Yesterday I had to get into my family therapy mindset, and I know it would piss you off if I did that every time you tried to talk to me."

When it came down to it, I didn't want to confide everything in him. Unloading my way-out-there insecurities and "what ifs" onto him wouldn't be good for our relationship. "I don't mind it some-times, but I think it would eventually turn our relationship into a mentor-mentee thing, and I like having sex with you too much to let that happen."

"Sex, huh?" He looked out over the water. "I was going to take you to see a movie, but we can skip it and have sex if you want."

"Or we could have sex at the movies." Where that idea came from, I didn't know, but it spilled out of my mouth before I could evaluate the you-could-get-arrested-ness of it. "I hear people do it all the time."

From his nervous laugh, I couldn't tell if Dylan liked the idea or not. "I'm not sure I could get it up in a crowd of people, especially if they can hear. You might be doomed to disappointment."

I was certain my shyness would take over and I wouldn't be able to follow through either. "I could just whisper sexy double *entendres* in your ear at key points in the movie."

This piqued his interest. "Like 'Can I put my hand in your bucket?'"

That didn't sound good at all. I wrinkled my nose. "Never refer to a lady's parts as a bucket. I was thinking something along the lines of 'Let me butter your popcorn.'"

"Referring to my balls as shrively, crunchy things is better?" He managed to sound both amused and offended.

"Well, when you put it *that* way…" He'd made his point, but I wasn't finished being adventurous. My brazen side could be used for good. "The park is deserted, and we're the only people in the parking lot."

It wasn't exactly private. Most of it could be seen from the road, especially since nobody had told the trees they should start sprout-ing foliage.

He put his arm around me and pulled me closer. "Getting cold?"

"Nah." I batted my lashes twice. Any more than that and I looked like an escapee from a mental institution and made myself dizzy. "You warm me from the inside."

The kiss he gave me was sweet and tender.

When he lifted his lips away, I whispered, "I want you, right here, right now."

"My ass is freezing," he whispered back. "Let's go to your place."

My newfound dream of risky outdoor sex was never going to happen.

Later that week, Daisy came over. She used to stop by sometimes when Dylan was unofficially living here so she could see her brother outside of practice.

"I miss you, Lacey," she said as she sat on my sofa and ate the last piece of German chocolate cake. Dylan had polished off most of it after I'd worked the frost off his ass.

I set a stack of napkins down on the table in front of her and put a glass of milk next to it. No coaster—I liked to live dangerously.

"You saw me yesterday," I reminded her. I'd attended the band's weekly meeting. I didn't always go, but this week, I felt compelled to drop in and let them know about my new company. They'd been as supportive as Dylan.

Daisy licked frosting from her finger, and I was struck by how long they were. She had that in common with her brother. The more I got to know Daisy, the more I realized how similar she and Dylan were, not just physically, but in personality.

"You're just like Dylan," she said. "He thinks seeing me for practice counts as quality time. Wrong. That's work. This cake is damn good."

"Thanks. It's my mom's recipe. We made it from scratch."

"Mmm." She closed her eyes and savored the last bite. "Audra doesn't bake. I'm so glad you do. It's good to have a family member with skills."

Daisy does this a lot. She treats me like I'm already part of her family. She treats Gavin and Levi the same way. That makes sense to me. With as much time as she spends with her band, they are her family.

"How is Audra? I haven't seen her or Monty in a while." It had been a week or two, surely.

"Audra is fantastic. She's about to publish a paper about addiction counseling, which she's hoping will help her get a permanent position teaching at the university. Monty is hopelessly in love with an eighth-grade girl who thinks he's the cute little-brother type."

Monty was in seventh grade. "She must have boobs."

Daisy laughed. "He's definitely like his uncle. Damn, I remember when Dylan was sixteen. I had to tell him that women could tell when he was staring at their chest. I couldn't take that boy anywhere."

One of the reasons Dylan likes sleeping with me is because he can snuggle his face into my breasts. At least he's overcome his staring problem. When I'm with him, I never see him checking out other women. He's been flashed by fans a few times, but I like to think his gaze lingered due to shock and not arousal. With all that leftover adrenaline, he was horny enough after performing.

"He must've been mortified," I said. "He's so shy about that kind of stuff."

"Staring at boobs?" Daisy chuckled. "No, he's not. My Victoria's Secret catalogues still disappear as soon as I bring in the mail."

I was silent as I waited for her to realize perhaps it wasn't Dylan stealing her skin magazines. She didn't appear to arrive at that conclusion, so I let it go. There was plenty of time for her to come to terms with the fact that her baby was growing up.

"I meant talking about it. And public acts of affection. I tried to get him to have sex with me at a deserted park or the movies, but he wouldn't." We'd skipped the movie and spent the rest of the evening creating our own private porno.

Daisy exhaled hard. "Yeah. Well. I don't know where he gets this prudish streak from, but I'm glad he has it. Otherwise, he really would be a manwhore. He gets propositioned at every single one of our shows."

I knew about that. I'd seen and heard it happen. However, he wasn't the only one who was the object of the fans' adoration. "So do you."

Daisy considered and rejected this. "By men. It doesn't count. Anyway, I came over to tell you I'm glad you kicked Dylan out."

I picked at a loose thread on one of my throw pillows. "What did he tell you?"

"That you said he was moving too fast. For the record, I told him that a long time ago. Well, after I told him he was moving too slow. It's like he doesn't have a medium speed." She gave a rueful laugh. "Please don't take this the wrong way, Lacey. I'm happy he's with you. I love you like a sister-in-law, but I don't think you should be in a hurry to make it legal."

I wasn't the one rushing toward the altar. Marriage wasn't on my mind, though I knew Dylan had definite plans along those lines. "He's a romantic."

"And you're a cynic. It exasperates him sometimes, but if he's going to be one extreme, it's good for you to be the other."

His romanticism sometimes exasperates me, but it's also one of the things I love about him. However, I do not consider myself an extreme cynic.

"I just thought we should date and get to know one another before we take a step like moving in together," I told her. "I know we were friends for a long time before we got together, but there were a lot of topics we avoided."

Daisy tilted her head to the side. "Then why did you let him move in with you in the first place?"

"I didn't. I don't even know when he did it, but one day I woke up and all of his stuff was here. I kind of flipped out and had to keep it to myself. That never ends well."

Now she rested her head on the back of the couch, though she still appeared to be giving me a crooked look. "Dylan's big problem is communication. He decides he wants something to turn out a certain way, and he does everything to make it happen. But he doesn't tell the other people involved what he wants. His first two bands fell apart because he'd do stuff without consulting anybody else."

That's not the way he'd explained it to me. "He told me Nadia resented the time he spent with them, and they disbanded because he was never around."

"That's partially true. It's also true that he would book dates and not tell anybody until the practice session right before they were supposed to perform. Or he'd rearrange a song and think giving a day's notice was enough time for everybody to make the changes. Kiss Me Goodnight works because we don't put up with his shit. We have a system in place that forces everybody to communicate. That's one of the reasons we have meetings every week. And we're also successful because you're managing us. Dylan sucks as a manager, and the rest of us hate dealing with the business side of things. It's easier to have you tell us what to do."

It appeared that Dylan's approach to our relationship reflected his general philosophy of life. Though I felt a little vindicated, I wondered at the inconsistency. "But he's a family counselor. Therapists are all about good communication. He makes me talk to him all the time."

Daisy chuckled. "Ironic, I know. He's learned a lot from having gone into that field. It has made him better about talking and sharing, but he only did it part time for a year. Audra thinks it's good that the music thing is working out for him. She didn't think he'd last all that long in family counseling."

Why would he choose a field that didn't suit him? Perhaps he'd sought to understand the turmoil losing his parents at a young age had caused. I've heard that most people go into psychology for personal reasons. I could see where Dylan would've felt adrift for most of his teen years. Though he had Daisy, she was probably focused on raising an unexpected baby and supporting the three of them financially. I saved that question to ask the next time I saw him, which was supposed to be later tonight. He was bringing pizza and a movie.

Another reason for his career choice occurred to me. "Maybe he went into it so he could figure out how to salvage his marriage."

Now Daisy gave me a really funny look. She scooted over and took my hands in hers. "That's probably true. It's also true that he's trying not to make the same mistakes with you. He was crushed when he moved all his stuff home earlier this week, until I told him that, despite his best efforts, he was traveling the same road. I blame myself. Audra and I did the typical lesbian thing. We brought a U-Haul to the first date. She came over and never went home. It worked for us. I think that's the example Dylan's trying to live up to. God, I hope I didn't fuck up Monty as well."

Of all of the Days, Monty was the most grounded. I extracted my hands from Daisy's grasp and squeezed her wrist. "I think Monty is the least fucked up of us all."

"I don't know," Daisy said. That ironic smirk was back on her face. "He keeps asking me if Dylan will pick him to be the best man at your wedding."

I shrugged. "He just wants to slow dance with Luma or Jane. They both have gorgeous racks."

Daisy frowned thoughtfully. "You're probably right."

Chapter Five

Over the next month, some interesting things happened. If you're like me, you'll want to skip the small stuff: I hung out with Jane and Luma; Dylan and I went on dates that did not include public sex; Daisy, Audra, and I took Monty shopping for clothes—that kid just won't stop growing. Now we can get right to a montage of the important things…

First, we signed Something Wicked:

Jane, Luma, and I surprised Something Wicked by showing up at their Saturday rehearsal. They used a soundproofed garage. Charlotte's father led us to the back. Henry was a tall man with blond hair and green eyes like both of his children.

From the way he looked at us, I could tell he was amused by our lack of age, which he translated into a lack of experience and a waste of time. I couldn't tell whether he thought his daughter's band was any good. When we got to the side door of the garage, he pointed a finger. "It's unlocked. Go right in."

The ladies were in great form. They didn't see us because they were facing the opposite way. And I was right about their normal appearances. Though Violet stuck with a black tee and jeans, they all sported makeup-free faces and ponytails. India wore jeans and a green button-down shirt with flowing sleeves. Charlotte and Bree had opted for comfortable leggings. This look worked, and I intended to encourage it whether or not we signed them.

India was singing a song we hadn't heard in concert, one that ended with a soulful vocal flourish I really liked. Once the last note faded, the three of us applauded and scared the shit out of them. You'd think four women making enough noise to have to soundproof a room wouldn't be so jumpy.

Hand over heart, Bree said, "We didn't know you were coming today. We thought you'd call first."

Jane grinned. "This is more fun."

"We don't have chairs for you," Violet said. "Charlotte, we need to get some chairs."

"We're fine," Luma said. "Keep practicing. Pretend we're not here."

I'd explained to Jane and Luma that I wanted to observe how the band worked together. I'd always been impressed by how well Kiss Me Goodbye handled their interpersonal relations. After my conversation with Daisy, I knew she was the reason it worked. She hadn't been in Dylan's other bands to keep them together.

I didn't want to put time and effort—and money—into a band that wasn't committed. This was an investment for me. I hadn't minded using my money for Kiss Me Goodnight's early needs, but after they'd started paying me, I began keeping track of my expenses and charging them to the band. The percentage I took from them was far below the industry standard. I couldn't do that with another band.

Something Wicked worked their way through the same song once more. They had an issue with the bridge. It took them a little while to actually forget we were there, but once they did, they brainstormed options and tried them out. While they didn't come to a consensus on the conclusion, I thought they did a nice job communicating with one another.

A half hour later, pounding on the door put an end to their session. Charlotte caught my eye. "It's Max's band's turn to practice. Did you want to stay to watch them?"

I shook my head. "Not now. We'd like to sit down and talk with you guys if you have time."

Jane and Luma had been on board with signing this band from the beginning. What I'd seen had convinced me I wanted to give it a shot too. They had real talent, they communicated well with one another, and I liked them.

"Sure," India said. "We can go to my house. I live next door."

As the yard had no fence, we walked across the grass to get to India's house. I wanted to take a paved path because I wasn't wearing shoes that would hold up to the slushy wetness coating the grass, but I was outvoted.

"I like this look." I pointed to their outfits as we made ourselves comfortable in India's living room. Her father was in the next room watching basketball and occasionally yelling at the television.

"What look?" Violet asked. "We're not dressed up."

"Yeah. This look." I waved my hand at each of them. "Beneath all that makeup, you have pretty faces. Show them. Your image is part of the package."

"You didn't say anything to the guys about their looks," Bree said.

"They weren't caked in makeup and dressed for Drusilla's funeral. Look, I have no problem with goth. I dressed that way in high school. However, we're looking for a band that's marketable. Like it or not, people judge you on your looks. If you're willing to tone it down, we want to sign you."

Jane handed out the contracts. "Read over these. We encourage you to consult a lawyer. You can ask us anything, of course, but you should have someone who's looking out for your best interests look it over. Call us when you've made a decision."

"Of course we want to sign," India said. "We're not stupid. You took Kiss Me Goodnight from nothing to touring with AFI in a matter of months."

"They're not you," Luma said. "You need to read the contract and make sure it's something you can live with. Working with a manager means entering into a partnership, and that's not something you should do lightly."

I think they were stunned that we didn't try to steamroll them. The three of us had agreed that we wanted to treat our bands well, and we wanted them to give informed consent. The fact that they were all young and still living with their parents underscored the need for us to be careful.

When we tried to leave, Charlotte grabbed my hand. "Lacey, please. You have to stop by and see the guys. They'll be heartbroken if you don't."

We didn't have time. I had a date with Dylan, and I needed to get ready. He was taking me to a piano bar. We were going to dance. I liked slow dancing with him. It was like snuggling in public, and that was as dangerously as he liked to live.

"Sorry. No time today."

Charlotte looked like she might cry. "But they started their band first. We only got into this to make fun of them, and then we found out how much we loved it, and…"

I glanced at Luma and telepathically told her to save me.

Luma patted Charlotte on the shoulder. "We'll stop by for a few minutes."

I needed to smack Luma or grow some better mental telepathy abilities. Jane and I followed her back over the wet lawn. My shoes were sopping, and my feet were cold. Even if the band was awesome, I was no longer in the mood to care.

This time, we didn't bother to be quiet as we went inside. The boys were standing in a circle, arguing about something. They stopped as soon as they realized we were there.

"Hey, ladies!" Bennett turned the flirting to about five notches above trying-too-hard. "Jane, you're looking good. Luma, breathtaking as always. Lacey, words fail me." He took each of their hands, kissing them as he schmoozed his way down the line. When he got to me, I shoved my hands in my pockets.

"Good thing you don't write the lyrics," I said.

Ari elbowed Bennett out of the way. "We changed our name to More Than Swagger."

Leo winked at me, a friendly acknowledgement, not a flirty gesture. "Like it?"

It had a catchy ring. "Yes. Now play your most impressive song."

They did. It wasn't one I'd heard at their tiny concert, probably because it was a cover of OneRepublic's "Stop and Stare." Covers are tricky. They either sound like a pale imitation of the original, or they change it up in an interesting way. More Than Swagger managed to sound exactly like the original, which should never be the goal.

When they finished, I shook my head. "Look, you have talent. Nobody's denying that. But you have issues with timing in your original songs. You need to iron those out before I can feel comfortable going to bat for you with venues and radio stations. Play something you wrote."

They played the finale from their performance. It still had problems with timing. I whispered to Jane and repeated myself to Luma. They weren't all that good, but they did manage to finish together. From the look on Ari's face, he knew exactly where the problem lay.

"We can work on that," he said.

"Okay," I said. "You have one week. We'll be back next Saturday to hear you again, but that's the last time. I want to hear your best five songs, and I want the timing to be right." I didn't hold out much hope, and I was tempted to skip the meeting altogether, but I knew Jane and Luma wouldn't let me get away with it.

(I managed to be on time for my date. I know you were wondering.)

Then Kiss Me Goodnight cut their album.

I didn't see Dylan much outside of work because the band was finishing up the arrangements for their album. It had a July release date, though the first official single was already available. In the meantime, Dylan had us moving in together by the first of May. Because he was giving me the time I needed to get myself together, I didn't mind the way he'd scheduled our forward momentum.

I was so proud of KMG. They'd worked their asses off and accomplished so much. A year ago, being signed by a major label hadn't been a vague hope, and now it was a dream come true. Not only were they incredibly talented, they were wonderful people to be around.

Levi picked me up and gave me a big hug every time he saw me. Gavin eventually helped me bowl a 102, which was a tremendous improvement from the first few times we'd hit the lanes. I was nowhere close to beating Monty, but I wasn't measuring myself against him. He could also dunk a basketball, and I was happy if I got it close enough to bounce off the rim.

Daisy and the band refused to transfer my contract to LJL Talent Management. They wanted things to remain exactly the same. I stopped asking when I realized they needed to see what LJL could offer them that I couldn't do on my own, and since I wasn't sure what that was, I shut up.

Soon after that, we signed More Than Swagger.

I have to admit I wasn't looking forward to seeing More Than Swagger again, but we combined it with a visit to Something Wicked. The ladies had signed a six-month deal. It was enough time to figure out if the relationship would be productive or not.

Jane urged me to sign More Than Swagger with the same terms, but I was adamant that a band who couldn't play together wasn't worth our time. However, I knew there was only so long I could hold out against Jane and Luma.

This time, Bennett didn't flirt with me. And he wore one of those earpieces that helped him keep time. I liked that he'd put aside his swagger to pay proper attention to his craft. It made a huge difference. The songs went off without a hitch. I liked them, but I didn't love them. I really couldn't see them making a leap to profitability, but one look at Luma had me swallowing my objection. This was *our* business, not mine alone, so I needed to compromise. If nothing else, I'd get to say "I told you so" in six months.

I turned to Jane. "Go ahead."

Despite my advice to look the contract over, they signed right on the spot.

"We read Charlotte's copy," Max explained. "We figured this is your standard offer."

In fact, it was standard for the industry. If we ever made it to the point where awesome bands were blowing up our phones, we could change the terms to something more profitable for us.

Let's see…what else happened? Oh, I landed Lollapalooza—the August festival in Chicago—for Kiss Me Goodnight. They'd be on the second stage in the evening, but I was in a good position to negotiate them to the main stage earlier in the day. After a lot of begging, threats, and gentle cajoling, I got Something Wicked and More Than Swagger booked as well. It was nowhere near the main stage, and it was early in the day, but this kind of exposure was better than nothing. That's right. I rock.

And Dylan moved back in with me.

It happened when I wasn't looking. One day, I woke up, and all of his stuff was here. The closet was once again filled with his clothes. Cereal boxes littered the top of my refrigerator. He'd shoved his things in various cupboards with no regard for my need to have things in groups of six. (Okay, *shoved* is a little excessive. He put them in neatly, but my larger point is that there were no groupings of six. No, scratch that. My larger point is that he moved in again.)

I loved him more than life itself, or at least it felt that way, and it hurt that he would do this to me. Our apartment hunting had been successful. We'd put down a deposit on a townhouse and paid first and last month's rent. Why on earth would he think I wanted him to move up the timeline? I didn't ask him to stay over every night, and I sure gave him strange looks when he came in late after being out with his friends or after a show I hadn't attended.

With two weeks left on my lease, I resolved to say something. However, tonight, Kiss Me Goodnight was headlining a concert at a bar in Grand Rapids. Normally I wouldn't go with them. The days of following them around everywhere they went were over now that I knew all the details that needed to be handled beforehand, and if KMG ever got to the point where I had to make sure they only had green M&M's in their dressing room, I'd better be making a shitload of money. Even then, I would tell them to suck it up. Candy is bad for you anyway.

I'm getting ahead of myself, and I blame Dylan. If he'd kept up his end of our agreement, I wouldn't be so fucking stressed out. And Daisy seemed oblivious to it all. She'd said not a word about the fact that her brother had moved back in with me.

Okay, where was I? Oh—the Grand Rapids date. More Than Swagger was opening for them. I'd wanted Something Wicked to take the spot, but India had come down with a nasty flu three days ago, and all the puking made her throat raw. It interfered with her ability to sing, and since I wasn't some *American Idol* producer/slave driver out for publicity and kicks, I substituted More Than Swagger in their place.

This was More Than Swagger's first appearance away from the Detroit area, so I wanted to hold their hands the way I'd done with Kiss Me Goodnight at the beginning. Since I had experience with this, Jane and Luma stayed home, and I did the traveling.

Ari was a mess. I found him in the dressing room pacing and talking to himself while Leo and Bennett watched. Leo tuned his violin, and Bennett beat his sticks on a practice pad.

"Where are Max and Bastien?"

Leo pointed to the hall. "Bathroom. Max pees when he's nervous. Bastien is nauseous. He's probably splashing water on his face and willing himself to feel better."

That was more than I needed to know. If he hadn't elaborated, I would've assumed they were washing their hands. That's where I'd be in their shoes.

"Great. Ari? You'll be fine. None of these guys have heard you. The worst thing that can happen is you suck."

Hands closed around my shoulders. I jumped and whirled to find Dylan behind me. He flashed his familiar smile. "Great pep talk, Lacey. She means that the audience has no expectations. If you can make the next half hour enjoyable, you'll earn a few fans. The people out there are just looking forward to having a good time. Give them that, and you'll be fine."

Looking over my shoulder at Dylan, Ari nodded. "Thanks."

"Yeah. Thanks," I echoed.

Dylan let go of me and crossed the room. He chatted with Ari, putting him at ease. This is one of the reasons I love Dylan so much. He's so good with people. In helping out a colleague, he was probably gaining another fan. And he made my job easier.

Bennett twirled this drum stick through his fingers as he came over to me. "We're going to wow you, Lace." He gave me a flirty grin and leaned against the makeup table. That position put him very close to me. The scent of beer rolled from his breath. He took my hand and lightly rubbed his thumb over my wrist. "You're going to fall in love."

I was about to pull it back—his move had definitely crossed a line—when I felt the palpable force of Dylan's glare. Looking up made me take a step back, and that put me almost out of the room. I hadn't seen him look that furious since he'd found out I was dating Thomas. Once again, I was reminded that I did not love the pissed-off look on him. It was scary.

"Dylan—"

He cut me off by pretty much ignoring me. Stepping close to Bennett, who was no longer leaning, he looked downright danger-ous. Bennett squared up to Dylan. That's when I noticed they both had strong jaws and well-shaped lips. Yep, I focused on the details that didn't matter. Things that mattered: Dylan was pissed, and Bennett was drunk.

"Hands off. She's your manager, not your plaything."

All things considered, Dylan's warning was far nicer than I thought it would be. Still, I needed to smooth things over without lying. I could totally do this by inventing some kind of tale about how Dylan was on meds or how he was super protective, but Dylan was in no mood to put up with that side of me. Besides, I was seriously trying to quit. I hadn't lied in a month. It was a noteworthy accomplishment.

"He wasn't hitting on me, Dylan. He's just flirty."

Dylan's jaw clenched a little tighter. "He was hitting on you."

Bennett didn't help matters. He poked his finger at Dylan's shoulder. "Aren't you the guy she socked in the nose in Ohio?"

I don't know how Bennett could know that. Dylan's nostrils flared, and I didn't want to think about what that might mean. I scrambled for damage control. "Bennett, tell Dylan you aren't interested in me."

Bennett didn't move a muscle, but he did sway. "You want me to lie?"

It worked for me. Time and again, lying had worked for me. Exhaling sharply, I switched tactics. "Dylan, back off. I can handle myself." When he didn't move, I slid between them. This put my ass against Bennett, which he probably liked. But I ignored him and focused my narrowed eyes on Dylan. "In the hall. Now."

The spell was broken. Testosterone spilled everywhere. It was stinky, but at least it was dissipating. Dylan let me pull and shove him into the hallway.

"Lacey—"

I held up a hand. "No. Dylan, why do you think I can't handle some nineteen-year-old boy who hasn't the sense he was born with?"

"I'm twenty." That correction came from inside the dressing room. Ignoring it, I closed the door.

Dylan glowered in that direction. "I came in to wish them luck, and he hits on you. That's not cool, Lacey. Not at all."

I crossed my arms over my chest to show I meant business. "Contrary to what you think, most of the world is oblivious to the fact that we're in a relationship. I know I said I posted pictures of us having sex on your Facebook page, but I didn't."

"You could have told him you have a boyfriend."

"Then he'll think he has a chance. He doesn't. He's harmless. I'm handling it."

A moment of indecision, and then the storm clouds in his eyes started to blow away. "Be firm, Lacey. You're way too nice sometimes."

I cupped his cheek in my palm, which was as close as I got to massaging his ego. Bennett had flirted with me from the beginning, and I'd never once mentioned having a boyfriend. Had I omitted that detail because I was pissed at Dylan for moving back in with me before he was supposed to? I shook the idea away because I didn't want to think about it. "I will. Now give me a kiss and get out of here."

He brushed his lips across mine. "If he touches you like that again, I'll wipe the floor with his ass."

"When did you go all caveman on me? Did you read an article that said women like these kinds of macho displays?"

He shrugged and turned away. "You used to be focused on just me and my band. Maybe I don't like sharing you."

I wasn't sure whether I wanted to be touched by his crisis or angry that he was being so immature. I didn't understand his insecurity. I wasn't the one fronting a band. My face wasn't plastered all over posters and the Internet, and no fans offered their bodies to me during and after performances. His reactions and behavior didn't make sense. Why would he think I could be tempted away? He could handle me selling liquor but not another band's music? I truly didn't see a difference. I had to schmooze and charm people either way. It also helped to ply them with drinks. If anything, I should be worried that the stress of being with someone as fucked up as me would drive him away.

I grabbed his arm and forced him to face me. "Is that why you moved into my apartment even after we agreed to wait until next month?"

His eyes darkened, and if I thought he was furious before, I was mistaken. "It's a couple of weeks, Lacey. What does it matter?"

Obviously it mattered a lot, to both of us for different reasons. "It matters. When I told you we were starting this company, you were supportive and encouraging."

He pressed his lips together, and I heard his teeth grind. Then he said, "I'm not talking about this with you here and now."

"Yeah, you are."

He ripped his arm from my grip and caged me against the wall. "I am still supportive and encouraging, but it seems like everything you do for us, you're trying to do for them. You're using my band's success to give them a leg up. We worked to get where we are. Maybe I object to the free ride you're intent on giving your new boy band. When does it stop, Lacey? When am I enough for you?"

He'd put his face close to mine and growled most of what he said in a low tone that wouldn't have carried very far. Confusion made me dizzy. The fact that Dylan was pissed and had me pressed to a wall didn't make me feel too good either. Some women like a forceful and domineering man. I equated them with people who were trying to hurt me. My rational mind knew he'd die before he'd lay a hand on me, but I wasn't operating in that section just now.

The panicked expression on my face must have penetrated his haze of jealous fury because he backed off. He ran his hand through his hair. "I can't talk to you when you look at me like that."

He walked away, disappearing down the hall and into the green room. That was good, because if he'd stayed near me after that comment, I might have punched him in the nose again.

Bennett poked his head into the hallway. When he saw that it was clear, he came out. "Are you okay? Look, I'm sorry. I didn't mean to cause a fight. I didn't know you two were together. I mean, the Twitter buzz says you're on bad terms, and the last time I saw you near him, you punched him."

My confusion still hadn't completely gone away. I stared at Bennett, wondering what the fuck he was talking about. He was so wasted that he teetered and fell against the wall. I wasn't sure *he* knew what the hell he was talking about. "When did you see me hit him?"

"I told you I thought you looked familiar. I used to live in Akron. My buddy's cousin managed a bar. He got us backstage passes, and we were going to the dressing rooms to meet the bands when we saw you fly at him. Someone shut the door, so I didn't see what happened after. My buddy and I decided not to bother them. We met the other three bands, though. Killer night." For the second time, he dropped his flirty demeanor. I wondered if he used it as a façade to keep people from getting to know the real Bennett.

I shook my head, not as a denial of what he'd seen, but to separate myself from that action. It wasn't my best moment. "Forget you saw that."

"Seriously, you could do a lot better."

I happened to think Dylan was pretty spectacular, and my heart ached over our disagreement. I could see the light at the end of the tunnel, but I didn't look forward to traveling that road. "You don't know what you're talking about. You can't judge a relationship from one interaction. Dylan and I were just friends when I — in Akron." And I definitely didn't want to talk about this with Bennett. "You guys need to get ready. Go find Max and Bastien. I want you onstage in ten minutes."

Before he could walk away, I grabbed his arm. "And no more alcohol."

Bennett wouldn't look at me, but he nodded. I hoped my message got through.

Part of me didn't want to watch More Than Swagger's performance. I wanted to find Dylan and talk to him, but every time I thought about the fact that he had celebrated how supportive I was of him and wasn't extending the same treatment to me, I just got angry. Being furious would only lead to sharp pains in my heart because I hated fighting, especially with him. Pile onto that the fact that he was jealous and had moved back in with me, and I decided staying away from him was a good idea. If nothing else, my conversation with Bennett had taught me to be careful of my actions in a public place. Who would've thought anybody had seen that private moment?

So, I found a spot near the rear of the venue and watched. I leaned back against a wall with my arms crossed over my chest. I hoped my bearing gave off clear signals for people to stay away. I breathed evenly to calm my emotional turmoil and concentrate on the band. They needed feedback if they were going to improve. So far, they'd solved their timing problem. The pessimist in me was waiting for it to reappear.

Before long, a woman came to stand next to me. She was a little taller than me, about average height, and the way she was dressed made me not look at her face. Her skintight leather halter bared everything above and below her boobs, and her skirt matched. If she bent over in front of me, I might be tempted to tuck a dollar somewhere. She might have been wearing bright red lipstick, but as I said, my eyes were drawn to the leather wrapping her body like strands of black licorice.

"Hey. Cute band, huh?"

I shrugged. Their swagger gave them a style that meant they didn't have to be all that attractive. People would be drawn to their energy and overlook their physical imperfections. Men sucked that way. Something Wicked would not be afforded the same luxury, at least not at first. Even Daisy faced occasional media comments about her badass sexiness. "Not bad. What do you think of their music?"

"Rockin'. Of course, I'm here to see Kiss Me Goodnight. They are to-die-for hunky."

Who used *hunky* in a serious conversation anymore? I nodded and tried not to wrinkle my nose in distaste. I didn't want to have a conversation with this stranger. "They're an attractive group."

She fake-smacked my arm. I hated when people did that. Then she *tsk*ed at me. "The lead singer is gorgeous. I'd do him in a heartbeat. I'm going to get backstage and see if he's game."

"You do that," I said. "But be careful. He's a jealous son of a bitch. Violent too. Once he decides you're his, don't think he'll let you bounce to the other members of the band. The keyboardist is an alcoholic anyway, and the bassist is the father of the drummer's kid, so that's not something you want to mess with. Piss off the drummer, and she turns vindictive. Just sayin'."

Holy hell. *Why* did I say that? Why? Can I get an "I'm kidding"? Come on, Lacey, you can salvage this. You were doing so well. One month without a lie is a great streak. Don't break it now, especially not with something so flipping *mean*.

Did I listen to the pleading of my conscience? Nope. I listened to that salving bit of peace rising through my core. It always accompanied my lying. I wouldn't call it a rush or anything so wonderful, but it felt good, and I really needed to feel good right then.

"You sound like you've been there." She probably looked at me, searching for a clue or a sign about who I was. "Is he good in bed?"

"In bed, on the floor, on the kitchen table, in the shower, but not at the movies or in a public park."

Oh, I chose *now* to tell the truth? Worse—I used it to support my lie. Yes, this was a tactic I'd used in the past. The best lies were those that contained truths. I was simultaneously disgusted with myself and growing detached from the implications of my actions. Was I becoming a sociopath? The thought didn't scare me like it should have, though my stomach was starting to become sick, so maybe it did. I was a mess, yet I still managed to carry my confident demeanor. Lying brings out the best and the worst in me. "He totally makes the jealousy thing worth it, but you should still try for one of the other guys. I hear they're stallions in the sack."

Blonde. She was a blonde. I finally noticed. Dylan isn't partial to blondes. He loves my dark hair. He would play with it forever, sinking his hands into its thickness or twining my curls around his finger.

"Maybe I'll start with Gavin," she said. "Bass is so hot." Then she shook her head. "No, I want the lead singer first."

I looked at her fully then. She wore entirely too much makeup. Her lipstick was blazing red. Dylan didn't care for lipstick at all. Her hair was straight. It fell over her shoulders in an over-processed and highlighted stream. She had a body that demanded attention, but the outfit would be a deal breaker for Dylan. "Pull down your halter a little. He's a breast man."

She thanked me and walked away, heading around the periphery of the bar. I watched her disappear through the door that led to the green room. Though she passed a security guard, he didn't stop her. No doubt her wrapping paper had short-circuited his brain. I made a mental note to make sure their next event had better security.

Chapter Six

Because Grand Rapids is a three-hour drive from home and we didn't want to be on the road all night after the performance, we rented hotel rooms. Dylan fell into bed next to me after the performance. He was exhausted, so we didn't talk about anything.

Guilt started eating at me as soon as I heard his even breathing, and self-loathing followed. I didn't fall asleep for several hours, which sucked because we had to be checked out by eleven and I was tired. Tired and heartsick. I wanted to go into the bathroom and cry while I washed my hands, but Dylan would've noticed.

It seemed I'd just fallen asleep when somebody began beating on our door. Dylan shot out of bed, a gorgeous, disoriented mess in sleep pants. He stumbled to the door and peered through the peephole before throwing it open.

"What's wrong?"

Daisy sailed into the room and yanked me out of bed. I'd sat up to see what the commotion was about, but I hadn't moved. Unlike Dylan, I wasn't wearing pants, only a long shirt. We had one outfit and two pairs of underwear between us.

I struggled to find balance, and Dylan pulled his sister off me. "Daisy? What the fuck are you doing?"

Levi and Gavin followed Daisy into the room. Both looked like they'd hastily dressed, and nobody appeared to have been caffeinated yet.

Gavin flipped on the light and handed Dylan his tablet. "She's justifiably angry. We all are."

My guilt turned to prickly gears churning in my stomach. I knew. The blonde in the tight leather I'd lied to wasn't the harmless bimbo she'd appeared to be. My lies had found a groupie with a blog.

I watched Dylan scan the screen. He scrolled down the page, and when he lifted his gaze, he nailed me with an all-too-familiar fury. He handed the tablet back to Gavin. "I'll take care of this."

"No," Daisy said. "You won't. I will." She turned to me, and I flinched at the pure hatred in her expression. "I know you've got some kind of problem, but I don't give a shit about that. Everybody has some kind of childhood trauma floating around in their backstory, but they deal with it. They put on their big-girl panties and get over it. I can't deal with your shit anymore. You're fired."

There was nothing I could say. She was absolutely right. I sank down to the edge of the bed and nodded. My insides were a special kind of turmoil, but I knew from experience that the internal overload meant my expression was probably blank.

"That's it?" Levi shook his head. "You called me an alcoholic and said Gavin was Monty's father. And that's nothing compared to what you said about Dylan. It's not funny anymore, Lacey. It's cruel and heartless. I would never have thought you could be so mean and vindictive, and you have *nothing* to say? Why? Why would you do this?"

I shook my head. Apologies mean nothing coming from me. They don't signify a lesson learned or mean I'll stop lying. I'm a horrible person, and I've irrevocably and capriciously hurt the people who mean the world to me simply because I wanted to feel better. That peace is fragile and fleeting, yet I have an endless supply of the pain I inflict on those I love. I folded my hands in my lap and gave myself over to the numbness.

"This is bullshit." Gavin turned to Dylan. "She called you jealous and violent. This isn't like spreading rumors about you being promiscuous. These aren't allegations fans will like. You can't shrug this off. She's getting worse, not better. What's she going to say next? That you raped her? Beat her?"

His words beat me, and I found I didn't know the answers to his questions. Was there a limit to the lies I would tell? Did I have any standards? I didn't think so, and that scared the crap out of me. It broke through the haze of numbness, and I felt pain.

"I'm sorry." It was all I could say.

"We're heading out," Gavin said, but he spoke only to Dylan. "If you want a ride, be at my car in fifteen minutes."

I'd driven in with the band, and it looked like they were leaving without me.

"You can't leave her here." Dylan's voice was quiet and broken. I closed my eyes against the pain I'd caused him.

"She can get a cab."

A cab from Grand Rapids to the Detroit area? I would see if Ari or the boys were still around. Levi, Gavin, and Daisy left. On her way out, Daisy stopped to have a quiet discussion with Dylan, but I heard only the hissing parts.

The door shut hard behind Daisy. She'd probably wanted to slam it but knew better since we were in a hotel and everything.

Dylan sat next to me, but he didn't touch me. "Lacey…"

I couldn't take the anguish in his voice. It caused an ache in me.

"I can't do this anymore. Gavin is right. You've made me your target. For some reason, you hate me. I don't know what I ever did to deserve this kind of treatment." He broke off, shaking his head. "I can't, Lacey. Do you understand what I'm saying?"

Part of me wanted to make him say the words, but the rest of me knew I'd been too heartless already. I nodded. "We're finished."

He clenched his fists, and I recognized the effort it took to relax them. "I love you, Lacey. I'm sorry."

"Don't," I said. "It doesn't matter anymore. Just go."

"Do you need money?"

I shook my head. He packed his things. I didn't watch. I sat there and stared at a line of dust crammed between the carpet and the baseboard where the vacuum didn't reach. I heard him pause at the door, but I closed my eyes. "Just go."

The door clicked, and I trembled. I hadn't wanted him to move in with me, but I hadn't wanted to lose him. He'd tried so hard to help me, to make me want to become a better person, and I'd resisted his every effort. Worse, I hadn't wanted to change. If I couldn't do it for him, I knew I'd never be able to do it for anybody. Dating married men had been a safe haven for me. They hadn't wanted me for anything but a break from their lives. My lying hadn't affected a thing because they hadn't truly cared about me.

I couldn't go back to that kind of life. Now that I knew what it was like to be loved and cherished, I couldn't see myself settling for less. I wanted Dylan, and only Dylan. My heart felt like it was being squeezed in a vise — an instrument of torture I'd tightened with my selfish compulsions. I deserved this. I'd begged for it, courted it with every lie I told.

Some sense of self-preservation made me call Leo to ask for a ride home. But he'd already left with Ari and the equipment. "Bennett, Max, and Bastien are still there," he told me. "They stopped for breakfast. Let me call them, and I'll call you back."

I showered quickly and packed my things, and I passed the rest of the time washing my hands so my brain would focus on the cycle instead of the wrenching ache in my chest. Twenty minutes later, Bennett knocked at the door. He was unshaven. His eyes glowed with leftover excitement, though the redness was definitely from a hangover. His first real gig had been fairly successful.

He took one look at me, and the smirky smile fell from his face. "Lacey? What happened?"

"I don't want to talk about it," I said. It was too tempting to lie, and I'd already done enough damage with that. "Can we just go?"

He looked past me, searching for the man who'd nearly threatened to beat him for touching my wrist. I was glad he chose *this* moment to be aware of the situation. "Yeah." He took my suitcase and herded me out the door. "Let's get you home."

I think they'd been in a celebratory mood before I joined their ride. I brought the atmosphere way down, so I decided to fake taking a nap. Before long, the boys were quietly chatting about how wonderful the night had been and the bright future ahead of them, and I was picturing all the ways I'd let Dylan down. Yeah, I was upset about what I'd done to Daisy, Levi, and Gavin, but my heart — as always — fixated on Dylan.

Max shook me awake. I hadn't planned to actually fall asleep, but the lack of rest and the oncoming depression had eventually killed my consciousness.

"We're almost home, but we don't know where you live."

I gave them directions. Bennett walked me inside. He hovered in the hallway outside my apartment. "Are you sure you're okay?"

From some hidden well of strength, I summoned a smile. "I'll be fine. Thanks for the ride. Rest up. Practice some more, especially those last two songs. I'll be in touch soon."

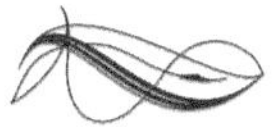

The next day came before I knew it, and I only figured out time had passed because the sun glinted in my eyes as it peeked over the next building. I winced and stumbled to the bathroom with no recollection of what had happened between the time Bennett had left and now. Blackouts like this had been fairly common when I was younger, so it—and the downward spiral that came along for the ride—didn't freak me out. Facing life knowing I'd never have Dylan in it, on the other hand…That stopped my breathing.

Not only was he gone, but if I couldn't turn myself around for him, I wouldn't be able to do it for anybody. Even if by some miracle I stumbled into somebody who could love me, I'd do the same thing: lie to him, drive him away, and break his heart. I'd hurt him and anybody he brought into my life, just as I'd done with Dylan, Daisy, Gavin, and Levi. Hell, this extended to Audra and Monty as well. I'd very likely become the first woman to let Monty down.

My suitcase sat in the middle of the dining room floor, still packed. I opened it and got out my toothbrush. It occurred to me that I should unpack, which I did until I came to my razor. I hadn't shaved my legs yesterday at the hotel. With Dylan gone, the exercise seemed pointless. I didn't care if my legs were hairy if I was the only one slated to enjoy them.

For the longest time, I stared at the blade, and then it hit me: that thing could take away my pain. It could solve my problem permanently. No more lying. No more hurting the people I loved. No more pain knifing through my insides. The feelings inside me now were unlike anything I'd experienced. Even losing John hadn't hurt like this.

I turned it over to figure out how to pry the blades from the casing. It looked like they should slide right out. With four blades in a row, one of them had to come out easily. Right? Wrong. I banged the damn thing on the bathroom counter. I got out tweezers and tried to pry one out. The fricking thing kept sliding off the blade. I hit the razor with the hard wooden heel of a shoe. Nothing worked. The blades were there to stay.

Disposable razor, my ass. The thing was built to last. As a last-ditch effort to salvage my plan, I tried to break it in half using brute strength. I was successful. Unfortunately, the broken blade slid deeply into my thumb. One look at the blood, and my head grew woozy. Too late, I remembered that the sight of blood made me faint. Getting my head between my knees wasn't going to be possible. I tried my best to control the fall. The last thing I remember was the floor hitting my ass.

I obviously wasn't going to be buying the farm this way.

I woke to find Gavin leaning over me. He didn't look real. Light glinted from his golden locks. I reached up and fingered one, trying to figure out how it got to be such a pretty color.

"Welcome back," he said. "Care to explain why you're passed out on the floor of your bathroom?"

"I can't find any bottles of pills." Dylan's melodic voice held a hint of panic. It broke the surreal feeling that had taken hold of me.

I lifted my hand to see if my thumb was still bleeding. It was. I glanced away. "Red, orange, yellow, green, blue, indigo, violet." I repeated this over and over as I opened the cupboard under the sink to find a bandage. Keeping my mind on the rainbow would help it ignore the blood. It was a trick John had taught me.

"Lacey?"

For a variety of reasons, I couldn't look at Dylan. Guilt was having a feast in me, but I had a more immediate concern.

Gavin took my hand. "She cut herself."

"Cut?" Dylan grabbed my wrist and pushed my sleeve up.

I took my arm back and got to my feet. It wasn't until I was rinsing the mostly dried blood from my thumb that Dylan realized I hadn't slit my wrists.

Gavin dried my hand and put antibiotic salve on my cut. Then he bandaged it for me.

Dylan picked up the broken razor. "Lacey, what happened?"

I glanced at Dylan because that's all I could take. "What do you think? I decided I couldn't live without you, so I slit my thumb, hoping to end it all." My tone managed to be derisive and dry. Dylan had once asked me to inject this kind of levity into my lies so people would know my statements weren't true. I hadn't done it before, but I did it now to make my truth sound like a lie. "What are you doing here?"

He shifted uncomfortably. "I thought you'd be at work. We came to get my stuff."

I nodded. "I'm late then. Give me a few minutes to change, and I'll be out of your way. Leave your key on the counter."

He opened and closed his mouth. I could tell he wanted to apologize again. He didn't owe me anything. I'd wronged him. This time, Gavin shifted uncomfortably.

I shooed them out and closed the door. I needed to wash my face and brush my teeth. They stayed in the living room and kitchen, gathering Dylan's things from there, while I changed my clothes. On the way out, I motioned Gavin to me.

"Make sure he gets his shoes from under the bed, and stay with him, okay? He shouldn't be alone right now."

Gavin blinked at me. He ran a hand through his hair. He did have a pretty mane. "What about you?"

I shrugged and lied lightly. The truth was no longer significant. "I've been dumped before. I'll be fine."

On my way home from that day at work—which, by the way, was one for the record books—I stopped to get some ice. Having landed three new accounts for Hanover Distribution, which would net me a very nice bonus check at the end of the month, I decided I could do anything.

In that vein, I took a step back and decided to approach committing suicide with the same practicality I used to convince people to stock my liquor. There was really no reason to continue living. Inevitably I'd drive Jane and Luma and my mother away as well. I was hopelessly broken, and nothing could fix me. I should've listened to my father when he told me to come out into the open so he could kill me the same way he'd killed my brother and stepmother. It would have saved so many people a world of hurt. My mom would've been heartbroken, but she would've eventually met someone and had more children. I know she decided not to have more kids because I sucked up so much time and attention. I'd robbed her of a good life as well. It was time to stop being selfish.

I'd always intended to donate my organs. If I wasn't going to use them, somebody who wanted to live deserved to have them. I wrote an email to the local police station and saved it in my "work in progress" file. In it, I detailed my last wishes.

No matter what, I didn't want my mother to be the one who found me. That poor woman had been through enough in her lifetime. So, I included the contact information for my apartment manager's office. She could provide a key to get inside. Then the police wouldn't have to break down the door and cost the complex more money. And the bonus I was expecting from Hanover could pay for my headstone. I admit my thought processes and priorities were thoroughly fucked up, but it was a good plan. My greatest talent would hasten my demise.

I'd purchased eighteen five-pound bags of ice. Ninety pounds would be enough to keep my organs fresh, and it was divisible by six. I'd fill the bathtub with them to contain the mess, and then I would take some pills—Dylan's was a better idea—and lay down in the tub. It solved all the problems.

Except once I got home and lugged all that ice up the stairs, I couldn't figure out what to take. I mean, I didn't have narcotics floating around, and even if I did, taking them would ruin my organs and then they'd be useless to donate.

Crap. I riffled through my medicine cabinet, and all I found was some Tylenol. I knew too much could kill my liver, but I didn't think I could OD on it. I stared at the mountain of ice in my tub. I'd bought way too much. The rest was in my freezer, the kitchen sink, the bathroom sink, and some was sitting out on my balcony. The nights had been cold, but I didn't know if it was still cold enough to keep it frozen.

Scratching my forehead, I thought about my options. I didn't own a gun, and though I was pretty sure I could buy one at Kmart, I didn't want to blow my head off. My mother would never recover if I destroyed my face, and no matter where I aimed, I'd ruin something on my head. Perhaps I should add a provision to my letter to the police to make sure they cremated me?

Disgusted that my winning streak was coming to an end, I wandered around my apartment looking for something deadly. Could I electrocute myself? I once saw a medical show where they followed a coroner who solves murders. They had a case where a man electrocuted himself with a sex toy that he stuck up his penis. I wondered if his organs could still be donated, or had he fried them?

I examined my television as I pondered this, and then I remembered the toaster. I could get into the bathtub and put the toaster in with me. Or the hair dryer. But did the bathroom outlet have a ground fault? Because then it would just trip the breaker, and I would end up bathing with a broken appliance. Once inside the bathroom, I realized my plan was destined to fail because the tub was still full of ice.

With a sigh, I decided to hang myself. I didn't have any rope, but I found a belt in the back of the closet. It was Dylan's, a discard from a pair of pants he'd purchased. He never wore a belt. Though he's on the lean side, he has enough of an ass to keep his jeans where they need to be.

I took the belt into the bathroom and tried to figure out what to do with it. Slipping the belt through the fastener made a noose, which would go around my neck, but how could I attach the other end to the shower rod? After careful consideration, I decided to make the noose larger. I looped it around the rod and put my head through it at the bottom of the oval. Since I was still on the floor, nothing happened.

So I stood on the edge of the bathtub and tightened the slack in the belt. And I jumped.

Did you know the shower curtain rod isn't always screwed into the wall? Well, I didn't. Turns out mine was a tension rod, so I ended up on my ass again — this time in a bathtub full of ice. It was surprisingly sharp and slippery and cold. I know I should've expected that, but I didn't. I'd expected to not feel anything.

I sat there with pointed edges of ice sticking into my backside, and I cried. These were the first tears I'd shed since Dylan walked out on me. I slid out of the tub and onto the ugly yellow linoleum floor, and I let go. I sobbed until it hurt, and then I cried some more. I lamented the things I had lost — Dylan, my friends in Kiss Me Goodnight, John — and the stupid things I'd said to drive them away. (Not John. I grieved for his passing, not for saying stupid things to or about him.)

I ran out of tissue, so I used my shirt to soak up my misery. After a long, long time, my sobs subsided and turned to hiccups. I crawled to bed without washing my face or brushing my teeth. In the grand scheme of things, personal hygiene could go fuck itself.

Jane called me the next day. I was on the road between appointments, so I picked up. She started by yelling at me. "Why didn't you call me? I had to find out from Levi that you and Dylan broke up?"

"It was bound to happen."

She snorted. "Oh, Lacey. Luma and I are coming over tonight. We're bringing ice cream and Twizzlers. As we all know, *stressed* backwards is *desserts*."

Ice cream was the ultimate comfort food, but I wasn't sure I wanted licorice anywhere near me. "Butter pecan?"

"And double fudge with brownie chunks. We know what you need."

"You're the best," I said, and I meant it. My friends were wonderful. I didn't deserve them, but they wouldn't abandon me, no matter how hard I pushed. That comforting realization came when I needed it most.

That evening, as I pulled into the parking lot at my apartment complex, I got a text from Dylan. *Can't break lease w/o ur signature.*

I stared at it for the longest time as it hit me: In one week, I'd be homeless. Last week Dylan had brought over some boxes so I could begin packing my things. I'd given up my lease so we could move into a larger place together. Breaking that lease would mean I had nothing. I whipped off a quick reply. *Don't worry abt it. I'll take care of it. Get ur $ back by next week. Promise.*

I had the money in my savings account. Paying him would mean my bottom line would dip below six thousand dollars, but I could live with it as long as I had a place of my own. My mother would welcome me back home, but I didn't want to live there. When I left, it was permanent. Going back would be like admitting defeat, and I had far too much pride for that.

Jane and Luma pulled up in their cars before I made it to the security door. I waited for them, eyeing the grocery bags they carried as they approached. Could I tell which had butter pecan by the apparent weight of the bag? My money was on Luma, but only because that was also her favorite flavor. Jane was a chocoholic all the way.

Luma made it to me first. She threw her arms around me, banging the bag into the back of my thigh, which was still bruised from my fall into my ice-filled tub. "Oh, Lacey. I'm so sorry. I thought he had what it takes to stick by you."

So did I, not that I'd made it easy.

They herded me upstairs with well wishes and sympathetic clucks. We had a ritual for these events.

Too gloomy for yoga pants or anything I equated with sexy, I slid into my fat sweats. Every girl keeps a pair of these because compounding misery is a critical part of the healing process. Normally putting these on makes me feel instantly better. I had my besties here to support me in my time of need—proof everything was going to get better. So, why did this simple act make me break down with body-aching sobs?

Jane came into my room and put her arms around me. "Let it out, Lacey. Let it all out. I'm here, and I'm not going anywhere."

"Yeah," Luma said from her perch on my bed. "Dylan was an ass anyway."

I disagreed. I had been the ass. "I lied, Luma. I said horrible things about all of them."

"You feel bad about it," she said. "This is actually a good sign. Usually you don't feel bad about the lies you tell or the people you affect."

I wasn't in the mood for looking on the bright side of anything. "Dylan wasn't an ass. He was wonderful."

"Bullshit," Luma said. "He wasn't as perfect as you think. He dumped you. That speaks to a pretty vast flaw in his character."

"Nobody's perfect," Jane said, which I felt only supported my argument that nothing extraordinary was wrong with Dylan. "Go ahead and start, Lacey. Name one thing."

I sniffled. This was the part where we cathartically bashed the offending party. I didn't have anything bad to say about him. "He left me."

"That's what started this," Luma said. "Plus I already said that. Come on, name one thing he did that pissed you off."

I didn't have to dig deep for that. "He moved in with me without asking. Twice."

"Twice?" Jane handed me the box of tissues I kept on my dresser. "Did you kick him out the first time?"

You'd think I would've told them about this, but I hadn't. Admitting it to myself had been hard enough. "Yeah. That was when

I told the station manager at their radio interview last month that Dylan was a manwhore."

Jane tugged on my hand, urging me to my feet and over to my bed. The three of us sat cross-legged on the mattress, facing one another. I blew my nose and considered washing my hands. I had a valid reason, but I knew if I started, I wouldn't stop until somebody made me.

As if she knew I was fighting my OCD demons, Jane cleared her throat. "And this lie you told a blogger—did that come after he moved in with you again without asking?"

"Yes. I guess he thought it was okay because we'd signed a lease on an apartment together."

Luma shook her head. "You'd think he'd know that you have very specific rules about the order in which things have to happen. That was a slapdick move."

"You make me sound so inflexible," I said. I don't think of myself that way. Yes, I have rules and procedures, but I think most sane and rational people do.

"No, but if you asked him to not live with you until next week, he should have respected your wishes." Jane picked at her fingernail. "I'm not saying you should've lied like that, but you were within your rights to be upset with him."

My feelings are always reasonable; it's my actions that are questionable. "He came into the dressing room when I was talking to More Than Swagger, trying to calm them down. This was their biggest performance so far, and they were freaking out. Bennett was flirting with me. I think he does it when he's nervous. Plus, he'd been drinking." I shook my head because it no longer mattered if some random guy flirted with me or if I flirted back. "Dylan came in. He was talking to Ari, giving him some pointers, but he took exception to Bennett's behavior. We argued. He was jealous of the attention I'm paying to the new bands. He asked when he was going to be enough for me. I don't even know where that came from."

"Well," Luma said. "We know what triggered your compulsion."

"I don't want to rip him apart," I said. "Yeah, we had problems, but it was my fault he left. I drove him away. Can't we just eat all the ice cream and watch *Steel Magnolias* or the season two *Buffy* finale?" Not having Dylan around made me feel like I had a stake through my heart. Why not compound my misery by watching Buffy have to kill the man she loves? Hadn't I done the same thing?

Maybe I should call these my drama-queen sweats.

Luma nodded. "I knew this was going to be different, so I brought two pints of butter pecan. Jane also picked up six bags of chocolate. She got the ones filled with caramel."

I smiled through the agony of my grief. "Those go great with butter pecan."

Chapter Seven

We had a sleepover. By the time Luma and Jane left the next morning, I was in a better mental state. I no longer wanted to off myself. My attempts had been pitiful anyway. But I knew that getting over Dylan was going to take a lot more than a night spent crying into my ice cream over Buffy killing Angel. I also knew my friends weren't going to leave me alone until they thought I was on the road to recovery, so I faked it.

And I threw myself into managing Something Wicked and More Than Swagger. I did what needed to be done. In addition to scheduling more appearances, I gave feedback that I expected to be utilized. Something Wicked had their act together, but women have to be twice as talented as men to make it in this world. They were, so that boded well for us all.

More Than Swagger was coming along, though not as quickly as I wanted. If they didn't get it together, in five months they might find themselves no longer represented by LJL Talent.

I mailed Dylan a check for his half of the deposit. The manager of the apartment complex wouldn't let me take his name off the lease without his signature, and I was too chicken to go to Daisy's house and ask for it, so I left him on the lease. When time for renewal came up, I could take him off or move into a smaller place. This apartment was set up like a townhouse. It had almost fifteen hundred square feet, a huge increase from the seven hundred and fifty-six square feet of my previous place. I didn't know what I was going to do with the extra space. It had two bedrooms, two bathrooms, and a basement. It had a washer and dryer in a closet off the kitchen. For the first time in years, I wouldn't have to take my clothes to a Laundromat or my mother's place to clean them.

I'd spent the previous week packing. Dylan hadn't been thorough in getting his things, so I boxed up the remainders. Jane took them to Daisy's house. She said Dylan looked tired, and he hadn't shaved.

He'd asked how I was doing. Jane hadn't unloaded on him, though she confessed to me that she'd wanted to. Instead, she told him I was spending a lot of time managing our new bands. I wished she hadn't said that, but then I realized Dylan no longer had reason to get jealous over the attention I paid to other bands.

My mom helped me move into my new place. She surprised me with a new living room group as a housewarming present. The main room here was much larger than my previous one, and it would've swallowed my single sofa and coffee table. This was the first new furniture I'd owned as an adult. The chocolate-colored sofa had two pieces. I could arrange them as an L or use them separately. As the set also came with a loveseat, I chose to keep them together. When the furniture delivery people left, I looked around and cried.

Mom put her arms around me. "You like it?"

"It's perfect." Nobody knew my taste like my mother. She'd even bought throw pillows to pull in the colors of the two prints I planned to hang on the walls. I sat on the loveseat and put my face in my hands.

Mom sat next to me and shoved tissue between my hands and face. "Lacey, honey, you can always come home."

She was wrong about that. I wasn't the same girl who had left for college at eighteen and never looked back. Life was still batting me around like a cat with a toy, but I was determined to fight back. If I took an objective look at the progress I'd made, I could admit I'd come far. I'd promised myself I would have a relationship with a man who wasn't married or otherwise in love with someone else, and I'd accomplished that. Dylan had been mine, and I had been his. That had felt good. Even though I'd never have that again, I could take solace in the fact that I'd once held the world in my arms.

"I messed up, Mom. I had the perfect man, and I couldn't keep him."

She rubbed my back like she used to when I was little. "Lacey, you can't take all the blame for it not working out. A relationship is about two people."

"He didn't mind my quirks. Even though I hated that he put cereal boxes on top of the refrigerator, he made sure there were sometimes six. He stopped me from washing my hands too much. He knew the signs that I was going to lose it, and he helped calm me down."

The hand on my back stuttered. "He enabled you."

I didn't see it that way, and her quick judgment made me mad. I wiped my face and turned to my mom. "He loved me. He accepted me."

"He let your behaviors dictate the relationship."

I couldn't believe she wasn't taking my side. But she wasn't taking his either, and that definitely mollified me a miniscule amount. I leapt to my feet. "He did not. He moved in with me without asking. Not once—*twice!* And he was jealous of the business I started with Luma and Jane. I was nothing but supportive of his band, and he wasn't supportive of me and what I wanted to do with my life."

Oh, I was on a roll now. I paced the room, and the fact that it was larger than my entire apartment had been made the walk gratifying. "He broke up with me because his friends said I would only say worse things from here on out. He gave up on us. I told him before we started dating that I was a mess, that I was hard to be with, and he said he didn't care, that he loved me. But it wasn't enough. It should have been enough. I didn't want to break up. We could've worked this out, but when the going got tough, he quit. He's a quitter."

My mom sat on the loveseat with her hands folded in her lap. She eyed me with a stoicism borne of experience. "And you did everything you could to drive him away."

I flinched. My hands itched. I backed up, intending to flee to the bathroom so I could wash them and cry some more.

"Don't you dare." My mom got to her feet. When Genevieve Zimmerman wanted to, she could be damned imposing. Her ponytail of auburn curls cascaded over her shoulder. Sometimes she looked so fragile and vulnerable, but right now, she was prepared to deliver a scathing tirade. "Don't you dare wash your hands, Alice Hollie Hallem. You've done this your whole life. You refused to let John adopt you or change your name. You wanted so badly to be Lacey

Zimmerman, but you wouldn't let yourself have it. You did everything you could to keep yourself miserable—and that was just the start."

Oh, that hurt, mostly because she was right. More than anything, I'd wanted to be Lacey Zimmerman, but I hadn't deserved that name.

I held up my hand because I knew she was just getting started. "Mom—"

"Do not interrupt. Dylan didn't respect your wishes, and he wasn't supportive of your dreams. You should be able to expect that from a life partner. But you did your damndest to push him away. I've heard the things you said about him. They were cruel, Lacey. It was a new low for you. You've always pushed people away. I've spent a lot of time with Jane and Luma, talking with them about why you do and say the things you do. You've hurt both of them, but they stuck by you because they love you. They're true friends, and most of the time, so are you."

Hot tears ran down my cheeks. My insides cracked open. Images of much better ways to kill myself flashed through my mind. I needed to forget the whole idea of donating my organs. If I was going to end my life, I needed to commit to the selfishness of it wholeheartedly.

"It's time to grow up, sweetheart. You and Dylan are both immature. Neither of you truly knows what it takes to make a relationship work. Given time, you can learn. I'm sorry this didn't work out the way you wanted, but it was doomed from the start. It's time to stop lying and washing your hands. Those are destructive crutches, and you don't need them anymore. You think you're not worthy of love? Too late. You're loved. Even Dylan, in his puerile way, loved you. He probably still does. There's nothing wrong with being inexperienced. That's where everybody starts. I'm not throwing stones at you, Lacey. God knows I've made my share of mistakes. It's part of life, making mistakes and hurting, but you have to learn from them. You have to put these lessons to use and grow as a person, or there's no point."

I sank down, landing on the edge of the sofa. I could have gone for the floor, but I realized my mother was right. I was being childish. Yes, it hurt. Yes, I wanted it to stop. But nothing I was doing was going to make my life better. Things hadn't worked out with Dylan, but that didn't mean my time with him hadn't been meaningful. I loved him. I always would, but losing him didn't have to be the end of it.

Daisy had been right as well. Shit happened to everybody. Mine was a little worse than the average person's, but it was still baggage. I needed to put on my big-girl panties and move on. For the first time in my life, my hands stopped bothering me. The constant, low-level buzz disappeared, as did the urge to wash them. I started to feel like I had before John died: I deserved to have a good life, one full of love and laughter, relationships and joy.

I was worth it, and for the first time, I really understood what that meant. Hallem had been my birth father's last name. I'd stubbornly hung onto it as punishment for everything that had gone wrong that horrible day. Instead of putting it behind me, I'd spent two decades blaming myself. My father's assholeness hadn't been my fault, and for the first time, I truly *believed* that.

I looked across the room at my mother, who waited patiently for me to wage my internal battle. It was too late to let John adopt me. "Do you think I could still change my name?"

She nodded, and tears wet her lashes. "John always hoped you'd ask."

I flew into her arms. "Thanks, Mom. I love you so much."

She folded me into a tight hug. "I love you too, sweetheart."

Two nights later, I was enjoying some well-deserved rest on my sofa while I indulged in catching up with some of my favorite shows. The couch was very comfortable, and I loved that I could stretch out on it in a variety of positions. I was flat on my back with one foot propped on the spine when my cell rang. Dylan's ringtone startled me.

The fact that I picked it up spoke to reflex and desperation. I'd turned a corner with my cornucopia of problems, but my heart was still broken. "Hello?"

"Hey."

At the sound of his voice, silent tears sprouted from the corners of my eyes. On the other end of the line, I imagined him shifting uncertainly, because I heard only static and the clinking sounds of a diner.

He cleared his throat. "I wanted to see how you were doing."

"Fine." I might have answered too quickly.

"Really?"

Even though I knew he couldn't see me, I shrugged. "All things considered."

"Where—I stopped by to check on you, and somebody else is living in your apartment. I drove by your mother's house, but nobody was there. Where are you?"

I snorted. Sometimes common sense deserted Dylan. "I didn't break the lease on that apartment."

A popping noise came from the other side. I had no idea what that sound could be. Then it got quiet. "You're living in the apartment we were going to live in together?"

"My lease was up. I needed a place, and this was available."

"So, the check you sent me—that was from you?"

I had essentially bought him out. "It was your half of the money."

"Lacey, I—When Gavin and I found you passed out in the bathroom, what were you really doing?"

He'd waited two weeks to figure out if I'd been trying to commit suicide? I wasn't going to cop to it. I didn't want to play that kind of game with him. "Being stupid."

"Lacey."

I knew what he was doing. He was using his patient tone on me. Hearing his voice hurt too much for me to get upset with him. "Let it go, Dylan. It was nothing. I'm better now."

"Really?"

"Yeah," I said as I wiped more freaking tears from my cheeks. I didn't tell him I was over him, because I wasn't. But I wasn't in a place where I wanted to end it all anymore. I'd even deleted the saved email I'd planned to send to the police.

A knock on the door interrupted my thoughts, but not my despair.

"It's me," he said. "Let me in."

I leapt to my feet and looked at what I was wearing. Dirty yoga pants and an oversized sweatshirt that used to belong to him and was currently stained with evidence of crying. I wore it more often than he did, so I'd kept it, and I was wearing it now because it was the closest thing to a hug as I was going to get from him. *Damn it!* I missed him.

Still, opening the door was a risky proposition. "Why?"

"Because I have to see you. I have to see that you're okay. And…I miss you, Lacey. I miss you so much."

I heard the catch in his voice, and I think that's what made me unlock the door. He stood there in his long-sleeved T-shirt and jeans, his face drawn and pale, staring at me. Did I rejoice to see that the breakup had made him just as miserable? No, not really. Having proof that I had mattered so much meant the world, though.

He opened his arms, and I fell into them. He held me with my face pressed to his chest as he moved us inside and closed the door. I felt simultaneously like I was dying and like I'd come home. Being in his embrace made me ache, but I wouldn't have traded this moment for the world.

I sucked in a trembling breath, and his hand was in my hair, tangled up and urging my head back. Without warning, he kissed me. It was hot and frantic, an onslaught I couldn't hope to resist. His fist tightened, pulling my hair in a way that sent tingles zooming all the way to my toes. I moaned into his mouth.

He broke away and sealed his forehead to mine. We panted in each other's faces, which sounds kind of gross, but it wasn't. It was wretchedly emotional. "Lacey." He whispered my name, a caress I couldn't resist.

I reached for him. My hands shook as I cupped his face. It was rough with a day's growth of stubble, just the way I liked it. "Dylan. I'm so sorry."

He shook his head. "No. I don't want to talk about that. I can't, Lacey. Not now. Just let me hold you. I need to have you in my arms."

I pressed my body to his and took his bottom lip between my teeth. Now that he was here and I'd experienced the unequalled bliss of his kiss, I wanted more than a cuddle. All those months we'd danced around one another, he'd drop a kiss on me, snuggle with me on the sofa, and then nothing—I hated that. I knew this wasn't us getting back together. I knew he'd leave afterward, but I needed to have him one last time.

I think he needed it too. He lifted me in his arms and carried me up the stairs. Wordlessly, we undressed each other. Sharp intakes of breath and heartfelt sighs were the only dialogue we needed. I touched him reverently, memorizing the dips and planes of his body and the shape of his lips, and he touched me with the same intensity.

We explored that way for the longest time, neither of us in a hurry for the end to come. It would, and we fully recognized that fact, but we had no need to rush. He kissed my body until I writhed under him, a panting mess of need.

Tears leaked from my eyes when he slid into me because I knew the end was in sight. He filled me, surrounded me, enveloped me. I drowned in this paradise, giving myself over completely. I had the largest orgasm of my life, but it was both bitter and sweet.

Afterward, he held me, stroking my hair away from my face. We both knew when the time came for him to leave. I put on a bathrobe and watched him dress. A million questions, many of them beginning with "What if?" swirled in my head, but none of them found release.

I walked him down the stairs and to the door. He looked around the living room, regret written in the lines of unhappiness underlining his mouth. I knew what he was thinking. *This should have been ours.*

He paused with his hand on the doorknob. "If you need me…"

He didn't finish his sentence, and he didn't turn around to see my response, which was good because I didn't have one. I needed him, but I couldn't have him. I'd blown my chance. I recognized that he shared the blame, but it no longer mattered.

Then he was gone.

The apartment felt empty. I couldn't get back into my TV show, so I turned off the lights, double-checked the locks, and went to bed.

The sheets smelled like him. I curled up and fell asleep. In the morning, when even that was gone, I doubted he'd ever been there.

Chapter Eight

I didn't hear from Dylan for a month, though I saw his car parked outside of my apartment a few times late at night. I'd sit in the window of my darkened room and watch until he started his car and drove away.

Something Wicked cut their first demo. They had three good songs, and I was working on getting them airtime on several college stations. More Than Swagger was close to having two songs ready. I wanted three before I'd start aggressively shopping them around.

Jane and Luma loved having a business with me, and the feeling was mutual. Having them around made everything easier. We were looking to take on another band, but once again, I was being picky.

I'd kept up with what Kiss Me Goodnight was doing. I loved their music, and despite everything, I was happy for their accomplishments. Plus, I still had all their dates in my calendar. I kept waiting for their next manager to call me for the itinerary, but nobody did. The several times business contacts or media had called looking for access to the band, I'd referred them to Daisy. If they hadn't replaced me, she was most likely handling everything.

So, when Dylan knocked on my door late one night, I was baffled as to why he'd be here. It was the night of KMG's album release. They'd shot a video too, but it was for "Wrong Name," so I watched it with the sound off. He should've been off celebrating with the band, holding chats with fans on social media. He shouldn't be at my door with a bottle of champagne.

"What are you doing here?"

He lifted the bottle and smiled, though it didn't quite reach his eyes. "Celebrating."

A fresh June breeze ruffled his hair like I wanted to. "You should be with Daisy, Levi, and Gavin. This is a big night for all of you."

"It's your night too, Lacey. We're here because of you." I shook my head, but Dylan pushed past me and came inside. He headed to the kitchen and opened cupboards. "Where are your glasses?"

I put my hand on his arm, stopping his search. "You're here because you're good and you worked hard. You deserve this. Go home and celebrate with your friends."

He stared at where my hand rested. "You used to be my friend. One of the reasons I dragged my feet so long with you was because I didn't want to lose your friendship."

We weren't at the point where we could put the past behind us and be friends. I let my hand drop away from his. "I'm sorry, Dylan. I can't. Not yet. Please don't ask it of me."

"Not a day goes by that I don't miss you so bad it hurts. I can't sleep because when I close my eyes, all I can see is your face. I was such a dick to you, Lacey. I didn't respect your wishes, and I didn't support you when you needed me. I hated the man I was becoming. That's why I left."

I didn't know what to say, but I did know to smash down the glimmer of hope in my chest. He'd said goodbye to me, and now he was apologizing. It was becoming an amicable breakup, though he was doing it in reverse order.

"I can't write. Not a word. Nothing makes sense. I should be happy tonight. Daisy threw a release party at The Majestic. As I walked around and listened to a thousand people congratulating me, all I could think was that you weren't there." He lifted his gaze and nailed me to the spot. "One glass. Celebrate with me. Then I'll go."

Pretty words. It didn't happen that way. One glass turned into two, and then the whole bottle was gone. I opened a box of wine (yeah, I'm totally classy that way), and we went to work on that. We eventually made it to the sofa, both of us stretched out on either side of the L.

Dylan petted the upholstery fabric. "When did you get this? I like it."

"Housewarming gift from my mom." I sipped more of the blush and watched the ceiling circle above my head. The pot lights moved so fast they were beginning to blur.

"You never wanted to have kids, did you?"

"Nope." I didn't have to think about that one. Babies freaked me out. Except now that I thought about it, did they really? Was this another of my crutches, like hand washing and lying, that I needed to reject? I amended my statement. "Maybe. Not six."

The song he'd written for me, a touching tribute to my fixation on the number six, had not made it to the album. It was good, but KMG had better ones. I didn't mind. I liked that he'd recorded a demo of a song just for me.

He chuckled. "Six is a lot. I'm not sure I want kids either."

I blinked in an effort to make the ceiling stop moving, and then I closed my eyes. If it was going to spin, I wasn't going to watch. "Unless you knocked someone up, that's not a decision you have to make right now."

"Knocked someone up." He laughed. Full-force guffaws shook his body. "As if."

When he stopped suddenly, I struggled to sit up. I needed to see if he'd passed out. I didn't have far to go. When I opened my eyes, he loomed over me. He'd crawled to my half of the couch, and he was crouched over me on his hands and knees.

"You're the only woman I want to knock up. But not for a few years."

With the tip of my finger, I traced a path down the side of his face. He winced when I poked him in the eye. "We had goodbye sex. I'm not going to sleep with you anymore."

"What if we had *hello* sex?"

I considered it. If we did that, we could have goodbye sex again. Then I shook my head. "I'm too drunk. If you lay on top of me, I might throw up on you."

"Okay." He nestled in between my side and the back of the sofa, scooting me over with his body. He slid an arm underneath and shifted me so we were spooning. "I've had too much too. I'm going to close my eyes for a bit."

The room looked better with my eyes closed, so I followed suit.

The morning sun glinted through the windows in the front and rear of the apartment, bathing the place in light. Dylan groaned and rolled to block it out, and that's when he knocked me onto the floor. I'd been aware of his movements, and I'd taken steps to catch myself, so I didn't land as hard as I could have. I'd have a nasty bruise on my hip to commemorate getting drunk with my ex and falling asleep with him on the sofa, but I was otherwise unharmed.

He snatched at the air.

"You missed," I pointed out helpfully.

"Sorry." He sat up.

I climbed to my feet and put my hand to my head. "I don't know if it was the wine or the champagne, but I feel like shit."

"Shower," he said. "Breakfast."

From his single-word sentences, I surmised that his head also felt like someone had been using it for a game of Whac-A-Mole. I looked at him. Except for the fact that he hadn't opened his eyes, he looked wonderful. I wondered if he'd truly been drunk last night, or if it was just me who'd imbibed too much.

"Headache?"

He washed his hand down his face. "Little bit. Want to shower with me?"

I shook my head. "Remember when I tried to apologize and you told me not to because you couldn't do this?"

He regarded me with clear eyes, the answer written there plain as day. He'd plied me with alcohol so that I'd spend the night in his arms. It was sweet. Low and underhanded, but sweet and touching. He nodded solemnly.

"I can't do this."

"Lacey—" He got to his feet and held a hand out to me.

"Baby steps, Dylan. I know I hurt you, but you broke my heart."

"Do you want me to leave?"

Unable to verbally articulate my response, I nodded. He kissed me on the cheek and grabbed his keys. Before he disappeared, he looked back at me. "Baby steps, Lacey. I can do that."

I exhaled hard when the door latched behind him, and not only because I'd been holding my breath when he'd smooched my cheek. I wasn't too full of myself to want his last memory to be something other than my morning-after breath.

With that last declaration, Dylan had made his intentions clear. I wasn't sure I could handle going through this again.

Monty stopped by the day after Dylan visited. He came on his bike. As a newly minted thirteen-year-old, he felt he was mature enough to make the trip. He stood on my porch with his helmet under his arm and a plastic water bottle in the other hand. It was empty. By my calculation, he'd ridden ten miles. It wasn't that far in a car, but on a hot June day…Then I realized he'd come from school. Scratch the ten miles. That was at least fifteen.

"Do your mothers know you're here?"

He blinked at me. "Hi, Aunt Lacey. I missed you too."

I gave him a hug. Yes, I'd missed Monty. He was a great kid. Dylan and I used to hang out with him at least once a week while he kicked our asses at everything from board games to soccer. On some things, I think Dylan had let him win. But with me, those had been true victories. And he used the title "aunt" with me, even though nobody had directed him to do so.

"You're bigger."

He'd put on perhaps an inch, and his thin shoulders had filled out a bit more. He grinned and touched his fingertip to my nose. "Maybe you're smaller. Are you going to invite me in? Maybe show me around? Offer to let me use the bathroom?"

I did those things, and when he came out of the bathroom, I had a cool glass of lemonade waiting for him. He sat down at my dining table (which was clear—I'm using the second bedroom as an office) and sipped his drink.

"I like that you have the fresh stuff. The powder is too sugary."

I knew better than to laugh at his attempt to have an adult conversation. "Glad you like it. Monty, please don't take this the wrong way. I'm happy to see you, but I need to know your mom is okay with you being here."

He shrugged. "I don't really care right now. I needed to see you."

"Monty…" How could I yell at him? Seeing him had perked my heart up considerably.

"I heard Dylan and my mom arguing. They were going at it pretty viciously. My mom's not someone who yells, but she can get loud when she wants." He frowned into his lemonade. "Do you have anything to eat? I'm starving."

As it was nearly dinnertime, I ordered two pizzas. Monty could eat one by himself, and if he was extra hungry, he'd start in on the second.

After I ordered, I sat back down at the table with him. "I'm sorry they were fighting, but I don't think it had anything to do with you."

He gave me an amused smile that he'd ripped off from Dylan. The boy idolized his uncle, and with good reason. Dylan would die for Monty. "Aunt Lacey, I know what you said about Gavin being my dad. That wasn't cool."

No, it wasn't. And here I was, being chastened by a thirteen-year-old. "I'm sorry I said that, Monty. I had no right."

He nodded, accepting my apology. I liked that he didn't hold grudges. His mother was exactly the opposite, but she had good reason to be pissed at me. I didn't blame her one bit.

Monty continued. "It didn't have anything to do with me, not directly. Mom was mad that Uncle Dylan left the release party. She said he sat there, being all dark and moody, and then he disappeared. He came over here, right?"

"Yeah." I wasn't going to lie anymore, especially not to Monty. He'd come to me because he was upset. He needed me, and I wasn't going to let him down.

"He said you should have been there. He said the only reason Kiss Me Goodnight got that deal was because of you. Mom said it wasn't all you, that they worked hard, blah, blah, blah. Uncle Dylan said she could deny what you'd done for them if she wanted, but it wouldn't make it true. He said Mom was lying to herself if she wanted to say you hadn't made opportunities for them that they wouldn't have had without you. They said lots of other stuff, some of it nasty."

He stopped talking and wiped his hand down his face. I wanted to take him in my arms and hold him like a baby until all his worries dropped away. Monty was too young to be burdened with this shit.

The doorbell rang. The pizza place was a five-minute walk away, so I knew it wouldn't take very long. I got the food and served my guest.

"Monty, I'm sure they didn't mean it. Siblings fight sometimes."

The look of disbelief he gave me was comical. He and I were both only children. "Mom and Uncle Dylan almost never fight. They discuss and sometimes argue. I've never heard them fight like this before."

And it was my fault. *Baby steps*, he'd agreed. Daisy didn't want me in Dylan's life, and if he was going to pursue a relationship with me, it was going to cause him problems with his sister. Daisy was more than his sister, she was his parent as well, and I hated the idea of coming between them.

"She said you were trouble. She said you turned on them after they'd welcomed you into our family. She called you mean names and said you don't deserve someone as wonderful as Uncle Dylan."

I disagreed with Daisy, but now wasn't the time to make my case, and Monty wouldn't be here if he agreed with his mother. I watched him pile three slices on top of each other and inhale them in six bites. I can't tell you how happy that made me. Dylan was the one who believed in crap like fate, but coincidences like this almost converted me.

"I was mad at you for what you said." Monty took two more slices. These he folded together like two halves of a sandwich. He guzzled the rest of his lemonade, and I refilled his glass.

"You have every right to be angry," I said. "I shouldn't have said what I said."

"Why did you?" He took a deliberate bite, and I knew he was hanging on my every action.

How to explain to a child that I'm a fucked-up mess? I tried the clinical route. "I have OCD. Do you know what that is?"

He motioned to my hands. "It's how you wash your hands all the time until Uncle Dylan makes you stop."

"Yeah." Close enough, anyway. "Well, I lie too. I was doing okay, controlling that impulse, until John died. It set me back a lot."

"And Uncle Dylan wasn't there to stop you from lying to that blogger."

I shook my head. This wasn't Dylan's fault. "It's not his job to stop me. I have to stop myself. I didn't. Worse, I didn't want to. Lying makes me feel better."

He stared at me for the longest time. I fidgeted, hating the fact that I was destroying myself in the eyes of a child who'd once looked up to me. He looped cheese around his finger. "I have this friend who used to start fights to cover up the bruises he got when his dad would beat him. Some of us found out what was going on, and now his parents are divorced, and he doesn't have to see his dad without a social worker present."

This time, I blinked. Hello, left field! It's nice when you stand up and make yourself known.

He waited for me to make a connection I failed to make. At last, he sighed. "Aunt Lacey, do you lie to cover up other things?"

Okay, his analogy had been straightforward. I opened and closed my mouth like fish gulping oxygen. I do lie to cover up *things*. Whenever my feelings threaten to overwhelm me, that's when I bring on the lies. "Yeah. I do. I did. I'm stopping again. I haven't told a lie since then, even though it's been tempting. This whole conversation, for instance, would be easier to have if I lied to you."

"I appreciate your honesty," he said. "Have you ever lied to me before?"

As I shook my head, I wondered if he knew I didn't lie in response to a direct question. "You don't stress me out."

With two slices still left in the box, he pushed it away. "After they got done yelling, they got quiet. That's when it's important to listen, you know? The things people yell aren't half as important as what they whisper."

The slice and a half of pizza I'd consumed turned to lead in my stomach. "What did they whisper?"

Did I want to know? No, I did not. I wanted Monty to spin me a tale about how Dylan still loved me and Daisy had given her blessing to him trying to win me back.

Monty folded his hands in his lap. "Uncle Dylan said your dad tried to kill you when you were a little girl. He said your dad stabbed your stepmother and your little brother, and he came after you last. He said you had to see them die and listen to them scream. He said you shot your dad, and he died, and that's the only reason you're still alive. He said you had problems because of that."

It never got easier to hear, even an abbreviated version. By the time Monty finished, I was shaking so hard my teeth hurt.

He flew from his chair and hugged me. It was awkward because he approached me as a child trying to sit on my lap to comfort me, and he was way too big to fit. Still, he got his point across before he gave up and resumed his seat.

"So, it's true."

"Yeah." I took a deep breath. "But it's not an excuse. I've hid behind it for too long. Washing my hands and telling lies helped me to not feel whatever I didn't want to feel. My mom said I had to stop using it as a crutch."

Daisy had said the same thing, only she hadn't been as nice as my mother.

Monty watched me with an unwavering gaze. His expression radiated sympathy and understanding. "My buddy stopped trying to throw down with everybody too, but it took, like, a year. For the longest time, he thought people were out to hurt him, so he figured he'd just hurt them first. Is that why you lie? You want to hurt the people close to you before they can hurt you?"

Perhaps the therapist gene had been passed from Dylan to Monty. In a few sentences, he'd managed to sum up a problem I hadn't been able to solve for most of my life.

"I want to stop doing that," I said. My voice cracked. I coughed and swallowed. Monty waited for me to get my bearings. "I'm finished with lying and washing my hands." I held them up. "They're looking better. This morning, I went to the bathroom and totally forgot to wash afterward."

Monty wrinkled his nose. "Too much information, Aunt Lacey."

I laughed, and so did he. At least I knew things were copacetic between Monty and me.

We chatted while he finished eating, and then I threw his bike in the back of my car and drove him home.

He turned to me when we pulled up in Daisy's driveway. "Can I visit you sometimes?"

I looked at the lights on in the house and hoped they hadn't been too worried about him. "You come clean with your mom. If she gives her permission, you can visit me whenever you want."

He turned a heart-wrenching, expectant gaze on me. "If she doesn't?"

"Then I'd work on Dylan. He might be more sympathetic." I knew I should've taken him inside, but I was a coward when it came to facing Daisy. One day I would, but that day hadn't yet arrived. I settled for watching until he disappeared inside the house.

On the way home, I cried again, but these were happy tears. I never realized how much that kid had come to mean to me. I hoped Daisy would let him visit.

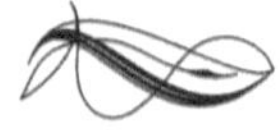

Three days later, I was perusing the slim pickings in my refrigerator when my doorbell rang. I wasn't expecting anybody, but I hoped it was the grocery-shopping fairy. I would fling open the door and tell her she didn't have to knock; she was welcome anytime.

To my utter un-astonishment, it was not the grocery-shopping fairy. I was dangerously close to becoming a nonbeliever.

The unexpected visitor wasn't Monty this time. He'd texted me that he was allowed to see me, but not until his grounding was over. Apparently he'd told Daisy track practice was running late. I hadn't sympathized with his plight. If I had a kid who pulled that stunt, he'd be lucky to see daylight ever again. Kudos to Daisy for not over-reacting. Monty's wings had been clipped for a paltry week.

The handsome man at my door today had buzzed his hair to nearly nothing since the last time I'd seen him. Light blond peach fuzz made me want to pet his head. His brown eyes sparkled a smile at me, though the lips curved up uncertainly. His light blue cotton shirt stretched across his shoulders, highlighting his broad musculature, and his orange shorts went all the way down to his knees.

"Hi, Lacey. How are you?"

"Gavin! I wasn't expecting you." I wanted to rise to my tiptoes and hug him, but I didn't know if that would be appropriate.

He solved the problem by opening his arms, and I leapt into his embrace. It was a tight hug — the kind you get when you haven't seen someone in a while. When he set me down, his smile was much larger. "Are you going to ask me in?"

"Sure." I inclined my head. "Come on in. I was just thinking about dinner."

"Do I know you, or what?" He scooped a bag up from the step behind him and went inside. "I brought Chinese."

It wasn't the grocery fairy, but it would do. Tinkerbell, you just might live.

"Oooh," I said. "I think I love you."

I showed him around my new apartment. At the end of the tour, he wandered around my office, touching things as he went. I had the usual furniture — a desk, bookshelf, filing cabinet — but I'd also put the sofa from my old apartment in there. It provided a comfortable place to stretch out and work.

"Are your new bands keeping you busy?" His tone was tight.

"They are. I have a small college tour set up for Something Wicked. It starts this weekend." Luma and I were going to accompany them. The girls weren't old enough to rent a hotel room. I didn't have many stones to throw. I'd turned twenty-five three months ago.

"That's the girl band?"

"Yep. They're pretty good and getting better every time I hear them."

We headed back down to the kitchen. Gavin gave me the whole box of chicken lo mein. He preferred to eat vegetarian when he could, which was why he liked Asian food so much. He was also a huge fan of Indian fare. He'd introduced me to some pretty outstanding dishes.

I savored my first few bites with orgasmic delight. Gavin laughed at me, but he closed his eyes and moaned a few times too.

"Why'd you shave your head again? I liked the sexy blond locks."

He shrugged. "Thought I'd do something different for the summer."

When he'd let his hair grow to a respectable four inches in length, that had been something different. This was more of the same. I didn't comment. "How are things going?"

"Okay. It's definitely not the same without you. We seem to be less busy."

"You should be gearing up for a tour to support your album." I'd planned the first leg of it, but then they'd fired me, so none of the follow-up work had been done. I wondered if the dates I'd scheduled had been canceled. "You need a tour. People like to see you play live."

"I know. Daisy's supposed to work on that, but she's busy with Monty. I think she doesn't quite know how to organize a tour."

A map of the U.S. and Canada unfolded in my head with all the major cities labeled. Booking a tour was a matter of making sure you hit all the major metropolitan areas, especially if they were also college towns. You needed to leave a few days of rest in the schedule, if only to have some flexibility with travel and needing to add dates.

"It's a lot of work," I said. "It took me almost two weeks to put together this small tour for Something Wicked, and we're just doing eight dates."

Gavin took a sip of his water. "Dylan told us about your problem. Lacey, we didn't know."

Suddenly my food didn't seem so appetizing. In my entire life, I'd discussed my past with exactly three people. I knew my mom had told Jane and Luma more than I had, but my friends knew I didn't want to discuss it, so they didn't push. They certainly didn't go around divulging my personal business.

Telling Dylan my secret was turning into a huge joke. He'd told Daisy. Monty had overheard, and now Gavin knew.

"Us? Who else knows?" I threw my fork down on my plate.

"Just Levi and Daisy. People you can trust." He put his hand over the fist I'd formed. I wanted to pull away, but I forced myself to stay put.

"He shouldn't have told you. He had no right."

"He wanted us to understand why you said some of the things you said. It didn't make sense. You were our friend — my friend — and yet you would all of a sudden start spouting crap. We didn't know what to think. I felt betrayed. We all did."

I knew I'd done damage, but this evidence tore at me something awful. "I'm sorry, Gavin. Really, I am. I've stopped again. I haven't washed my hands all week, except for when I should, and I haven't lied since that night. I'm trying. I know it's too late. I don't expect forgiveness."

He crooked his finger under my chin and lifted it until I faced him. "You have it."

"But it's not an excuse, not anymore. Maybe when I was little, it was a defense I needed, but now it only hurts the people I love."

Gavin sighed. "Stop, Lacey. I've forgiven you and moved past it. I want us to be friends again. I'm not saying come back and manage the band, but I miss having you in my life. You were getting to be such a good bowler, almost good enough to be on my team."

I had to laugh at that. Gavin and Monty had regularly been on the winning team, while Dylan, Luma, and I had become used to having the floor wiped with our asses. Dylan had even bought me a pair of bowling shoes so I wouldn't have to rent those disgusting things that thousands of people had worn before me. That man and shoes…

"I do miss bowling." Not the actual sport, but the part where I got to hang out with friends, drink watery beer, and make jokes about messing around with balls. I took a bite of my lo mein. Maybe it wasn't so bad having people know about my past. They didn't seem to be judging me. Gavin stayed late that night, and I let him kick my ass at Wii bowling just to show what a good sport I could be. He left me with a hug and an invitation to bowl with him (for real) the following week.

My life was far from back to normal, but it was getting better—my friends were proving they were made of strong stuff. Levi showed up after eight two nights later with a case of beer and a grin. "Want to be an alcoholic with me?"

We played quarters. I had a bunch of small plastic cups, which we set out in a pyramid on the dining room table and filled with beer. Levi washed a quarter, and then we flipped it to see who went first.

The game is more difficult than it appears. The more we played, the better we got at aiming for and landing in a cup. Then we reached the point where no amount of talent was going to improve our aim.

"I like that we didn't have to have a big discussion about everything," I said after I'd missed the cup for which I'd aimed and had to guzzle it down.

Levi nodded sagely. "We're good like that. I noticed from the start that you save the worst lies for Dylan when he's pissed you off."

That had been the long and the short of it. I matched his sagacity with my tone, if not the substance of my words. "Sometimes he pisses me off."

"He's like that. I've known him since we were in middle school. He was popular. All the girls wanted to date him. I was a skinny geek with thick glasses and braces. We weren't friends. He used to copy my math homework. It pissed me off, and I told him to stop."

This was the first time Levi had opened up and talked to me about knowing a younger Dylan. I knew they hadn't been friends. I leaned forward and spilled two cups of beer. "Did he stop?"

Levi thought for a minute. "He must have. I don't remember talking to him again until our senior year of high school when he wanted to form a band. He'd heard I played piano, so he wanted me to play keyboard."

I didn't remember Dylan saying Levi had been in a band with him before. "Did you?"

"Nope. He was still full of himself, the kind of person who thought I'd be so honored to have been asked that I'd drop everything and be available. I told him he was kind of a jerk and being in a band would interfere with my LARPing schedule. I was a Knight of the Round Table."

Picturing Levi dressed up as a medieval knight wandering through the woods with a plastic sword made me crack up. I laughed so hard I knocked over three more cups of beer.

Levi pushed me out of the way and sopped up my mess with paper towels. "Let me rescue your table and floor, my fair lady."

Fascinated by the way the paper towels absorbed the liquid, I watched Levi work. It got really quiet, a comfortable silence between friends. Then I broke it suddenly. "I was the crazy quiet girl dressed in all black who hated everybody and everything."

He put the sopping towels in the trash and washed his hands. "Camouflage. Everybody hides in high school. I hid behind a suit of armor, Dylan hid behind his band—which never did perform—and you hid behind goth clothes."

I'd hidden a long time. My camo had changed, morphing into hand washing and lying, but it had saved me from—or at least kept me from—so many potentially messy emotional entanglements. But lowering my shield to let these guys in was the best thing I'd ever done.

"So wise. I do love you, Levi. And I'm not hiding anymore."

He threw a cute grin my way. "Me neither. I can't speak for anybody else, though."

I wondered if Dylan was still hiding. And why?

Chapter Nine

Meet me @11:30

Dylan's text came with an address and no time to plan an outfit or grab lunch before I ran out to meet him. I did question the wisdom of dropping everything to see my ex-boyfriend, but I didn't spend much time analyzing why I wanted to go. The last time he spent the night, we'd left things on a positive note. I wasn't sure what "baby steps" entailed or promised, but this was probably it.

I put the address into my GPS. It took me to the coffee shop where we'd first met, and my heart melted. Through the window, I could see Dylan sitting at the same seat he'd selected when he'd stopped by to grab coffee with Audra and Monty after one of Audra's softball practices.

The chair where I'd been was empty. Dylan's attention was on his phone when I came in and jangled the bell on the door. He looked up, and his face lit when he saw me.

He got to his feet. I liked when a man stood up to greet me. It spoke of respect and old-world manners. And Dylan had that extra added dash of I-want-to-get-into-your-pants that I found irresistible. I wanted to get into his pants too, but I knew the value of waiting until we were both ready.

"You got my text."

Suddenly I realized I hadn't replied. I'd used the time to brush my teeth and fix my hair. I'd been working from home that morning, and I didn't have to look great to do it. At least I knew Dylan liked the way I looked in yoga pants and a jogging shirt.

I gave my wardrobe a cursory glance. "And I rushed here."

He kissed my cheek. "You look amazing."

That deserved a snort. "You're easy."

Wearing his AFI *Black Sails* shirt and worn-out jeans, *he* looked amazing. This was the same outfit he'd sported the first time I laid eyes on him. He laughed at my reply. "I aim to please."

He pulled a chair out for me. "This is a modified version of our first date."

"It wasn't a first date. It's the day we met."

"It should have been a date."

We sat. Reaching under the table, he grabbed something. Paper rattled, and then he set a Jimmy John's bag in front of me. "Ham and cheese."

"You remember what I was eating?"

"I remember everything. You were wearing a dark gray skirt and a white button-down blouse with a V-neck. Whenever I glanced over, I could see the curve of your boob."

Oh, that had to have made his day.

"Shoes?" He did like shoes, but even I didn't remember what I'd been wearing.

"Low-heeled black pumps. You threw them out a few months ago because the toe was wearing out."

Through his superior smirk, a significant moment passed between us. I remembered what Levi had said about Dylan always taking people for granted. I don't think he meant to, and this was a step toward him turning over a new leaf.

"Did you invite Audra and Monty?"

"Nope. This time, it's just you and me." He winked. "I was going to get you an iced latte, but you haven't had one in a long time. Do you want a chai tea?"

That sounded heavenly. It might be the middle of July outside, but in Michigan, that didn't mean warm weather. This week was decidedly chilly. He deduced my answer from my body language.

"I'll be right back."

I watched him go, admiring his assets all the way to the counter and back.

When he set the tea down in front of me, he said, "You watched me that same way the first time. The place was crowded, and when Monty and I came to claim the seats by you, I tried not to check you out too openly. Monty was at a stage where he thought it was funny to call audibles whenever he thought I might be attracted to a woman."

I could easily picture Monty doing that. "Oh Lord. I probably would've been in the bathroom much sooner. He might have saved you from having coffee spilled all over your lap."

"I wouldn't change that for anything. For the next week, every time I smelled coffee, images of your face bombarded me. I cursed myself for not getting your number. Running into you again was fate, Lacey."

I glanced away. He knew my opinion about fate and destiny.

He touched the back of my hand, bringing my attention to him. "I want to make this our first date. Let's pretend like we just met."

My jaw dropped. "But you bought me lunch and kissed my cheek. Strangers don't do that for each other." A shiver went through me. "Can we meet in the bathroom and have illicit sex?"

From the expression on his face, that hadn't been the reaction he pictured. I'm not sure he knew how to respond.

"Never mind. Pretend I didn't say that." I stuck out my hand. "Hi. I'm Lacey Zimmerman. Do you come here often?"

He stared at my hand, and I knew what he was thinking. For the past six weeks, Dylan, Monty, Gavin, and Levi had been visiting me. They stopped by in pairs or singly, and we always hung out for a few hours, discussing anything and everything except music and Daisy. Dylan and I hadn't done anything that might be construed as dating. There had been no stolen kisses, no holding hands or snuggling as we watched TV.

Not once had I mentioned changing my name.

"Go ahead. I won't bite until I know you better."

The internal struggle lost to his desire to go along with his original plan. "I'm Dylan. It's nice to meet you, Lacey. Do you mind if I sit with you?"

"I'd love the company." I moved my sandwich wrapper to the side to make room. "Are you from around here? I used to be, but I moved recently. Now this place is a little out of the way, but today it's worth the drive."

"I agree," he said. "I don't live that close, but I was in the neighborhood. Lacey is an interesting name. I don't think I've met anybody with that name before."

I knew what he was fishing for, but I was having too much fun to give in. "I know four people named Dylan. One was friends with my stepfather. He passed away—my stepfather, not his friend. His son is also Dylan. Then there was this boy in my Spanish class in high school, and—Oh! My first boyfriend was named Dylan."

Now I'd truly baffled him. "Stepfather?"

"Yeah. His name was John. He was awesome. He always wanted to adopt me, but now I'm too old, so I just changed my name to his. Same thing, right?"

For a second, Dylan's act dropped. "You really changed your name?"

"I did. Want to see my driver's license?" Since I knew he'd want proof that Alice Hollie Hallem no longer existed, I was already whipping it out. There, with a fresh photo of me, was my new name: Lacey Zimmerman.

He studied it. "No middle name?"

"Hell, no. It's perfect as is."

He handed it back. "That's a big step. I'm proud of you."

Seeing my new name would never get old. I gave my little card one more pleased glance before I tucked it away. "What about you? What's the biggest change you've ever made in your life?"

He sipped his coffee and thought about that one. "Waking up alone."

While I hadn't expected that answer, I understood where it had come from. Dylan was a snuggler. He liked to fall asleep with me in his arms, and if we somehow separated during the night, he always managed to have part of his body touching mine.

I took a bite of my sandwich. "Maybe you'll meet somebody someday soon, fall in love, and then after an acceptable dating period, she'll want you to move in with her."

With his laugh, the pall his admission had cast over us vanished. "Maybe. So, what's your favorite color?"

"Teal." My shy smile accompanied that answer.

"Yeah? Mine's cherry red."

At that, my blush deepened. I wasn't much of a blusher, and Dylan usually liked to make the most of it when I did. This time, he didn't.

"Favorite cover song."

I know he wanted me to say the version of "Endlessly, She Said" that Kiss Me Goodnight did, but that would be a lie. "KMFDM's cover of 'Crazy Horses.' I find it ironic that an industrial band covered The Osmonds."

The ice broke after that. We'd put our most important pieces of news on the table, and now we moved to other topics. He peppered me with questions, and I did the same to him. We asked questions with answers we knew, but we also managed to ask a surprising number of new things. I found out he knows how to play the trumpet and the piano, though he dislikes both. He found out my favorite number isn't six. (It's thirty-six.)

I liked going back and starting anew. It was refreshing. The pressure I'd felt before, even with the promise of "baby steps," vanished. This felt right. We sat there for three hours, laughing, joking, chatting, and getting to know one another.

When I had to leave, he said, "I had fun. I'd like to see you again."

"I'd like that too."

"How about this weekend? They're showing a movie in the park. We could bring a cooler and watch it under the stars."

This weekend was bad for me. I dropped the façade of having just met him. He did as well. "Something Wicked is doing a college tour. They leave the day after tomorrow, and we'll be gone for two weeks. Luma and I are going with them."

Jane still worked for a law firm. She couldn't take off like Luma and I could.

Dylan's face fell. "Oh. Two weeks. That's a long time. Is More Than Swagger going as well?"

I knew what he was fishing for. He would never like Bennett. That's okay. I wasn't too fond of him either. "No. They're not progressing the way I'd hoped. They're not ready for a tour."

That news placated him a little. "How about when you get back?"

"Absolutely. I'll call you. We can set something up."

He walked me to my car. Just when I thought he was going to let me go with another peck on the cheek, he captured my lips. His arms enveloped my body while he worked his magic. My lips tingled, and I felt the vibrations all the way to my knees. It was a good thing he was there to support me, otherwise I might have sunk to the ground and become a puddle of goo. Then, as suddenly as it began, the kiss was over. He looked down at me, a cocky-ass grin on his face.

This was classic Dylan. Kiss me breathless and pretend like it was nothing. And then I realized something fundamental about this man: once he decided he wanted something, he took it. This was supposed to be our second first kiss. He didn't bother with a tentative foray — he didn't even ask — he just dove in and smacked me with his best shot. It explained why he'd moved in with me twice without stopping to ask. He'd wanted to make a life with me, so he went ahead and did it.

Even though he's infuriating, I absolutely love this man.

I wobbled as I opened my car door. Dylan steadied me.

"You okay?"

I was perfect. Understanding the situation gave me insight, and it made the idea of getting back together with him that much more appealing. I slid into my seat. "Peachy."

I know for a fact that I partied hard in college. But what I saw on tour with Something Wicked made me doubt memories of my stamina. The members of Something Wicked were underage, and Luma warned them away from drinking, if only so that unsavory rumors wouldn't get started. They were young, and we needed them to be seen as responsible. If a group could make good decisions when they were young and the pressure to let loose was on, it was a safe bet they were reliable enough for a long-term investment.

At two different points along the tour (and I wouldn't tell them which ones), I had recording industry scouts scheduled to be in attendance, and I hoped they showed up. One was a man who'd shown interest in Kiss Me Goodnight, but the band had chosen another label. I'd developed him as a contact through Patrick Westman, whom I'd met through Thomas. (You remember Thomas — handsome, rich ex-boyfriend with the goatee?) The other was from a smaller label. Neither of them was a sure thing.

Anyway, I can't remember ever seeing so many college students wasted like this. Perhaps that's because when I'd been in a position to notice, I'd been just as inebriated? I thought wistfully about how nice it would be to let the spirits take me where they might. In the end, I settled for just enjoying the amount of men who hit on me. It's a good thing Dylan wasn't there. His possessive streak definitely showed up when he wasn't certain everything was kosher between us, and considering that we'd hit the reset button, things weren't to the point where he would feel like I belonged to him and nobody else.

I did, of course. My heart was feverishly rooting for him to win, and my head appreciated having this time to catch up.

Out of professional courtesy, I'd invited Patrick Westman to the Boston show. I'd sent him an email that said I would leave four tickets for him at Will Call, which I did. I hoped he'd show up. He had connections in the business, and I wanted as many people to see Something Wicked as possible. I did not expect him to show up with Thomas in tow.

Something Wicked was the second opening act for the main event, a band out of Ireland called Two Door Cinema Club that was making waves across the alternative rock scene. Luma and I were at a table in the back waiting for Something Wicked to come on. We'd avoided going backstage for the past hour because we wanted the girls to have a little more freedom so we could see what they'd do with it. I don't think we started out thinking we'd be as controlling as we were. Perhaps if the bands we managed weren't so young, we could've relaxed a bit. Kiss Me Goodnight had never needed me this much for a show, though I'd stayed with them because they were my friends. And I'd been bumping uglies with the lead singer.

So, we were sitting there, nursing our one drink of the evening, when Luma elbowed me hard. (I have a bruise on my arm to prove it. So *there*, Luma. I'm going to post pictures on my Facebook page so people can see how violent you really are.) My first reaction was a strong urge to kick her in the shin, but when I glared at her, she started nodding frantically at some point over my shoulder. I turned around in time to see Patrick lift his hand in greeting. He navigated through the crowd, and that's when I saw who else he'd brought: Steve, his boyfriend, followed him, and Thomas brought up the rear.

I'm sure my eyes were as wide as saucers. I hadn't seen or heard from Thomas since he'd broken up with me the day after John's funeral. That sounds like he's heartless, and he's really not. I'd been too grief-stricken to hide my feelings for Dylan, and Thomas had too much self-respect to stay with a woman who was so obviously in love with another man. But he'd been there for me throughout the funeral, and he'd looked after me until the next morning.

He looked good, but not great. Though he wore a suit — his one concession to the informality of the event meant he'd left his jacket at home — something about him was off. As he came closer, I kept staring, trying to figure out what was wrong.

Patrick greeted me with a kiss on the cheek. Steve followed the same way. Thomas enveloped me with a huge hug, which I wholeheartedly returned. I'd missed his companionship.

"Lacey, you look great. How're you doing?" He spoke in a low tone near my ear, and I realized the problem. He looked like he hadn't been sleeping. Either that, or he'd been ill.

"I'm okay, Thomas. How are *you* doing?"

He released me, laughing. "I am fine. Or rather, I will be." He gestured to my chair, indicating that I should sit. "Hi, Luma. How have you been?"

She smiled, not really covering her alarm at having Thomas in the same place as me. I didn't see the problem. Even if I hadn't been over the moon for Dylan, my relationship with Thomas wasn't one that would ever be rekindled.

He greeted her with the same heartfelt hug. When the dust settled, Thomas sat on the other side of me, with Patrick next to Luma. Steve was between Patrick and Thomas, though I had kind of hoped he'd end up nearer to me. You see, Steve is an executive at Virgin. While he didn't actively scout talent, he had the power to make or break careers. I wanted Something Wicked to wow him.

Under the table, I squeezed Luma's hand. I knew we were both praying our girls knocked it out of the park.

Thomas ordered a whiskey. While I'd seen him drink before, he usually kept it to lighter fare. I guess he was really off the clock tonight. No need to stay in control when there was nobody to impress.

"What have you been up to?" I sincerely wanted to know how he'd been. He was a sweet man, and he'd been an excellent boyfriend.

He swirled his drink and lifted a shoulder. "Do you really want to know?"

I gave him a lopsided smile. "I really want to know."

"On the plane ride back from seeing you that last time, I met someone. We clicked, kind of like the way you did with Dylan. It was amazing."

My lopsided smile came out full force. "That's wonderful. I'm so happy for you. Will she be here tonight? I left four tickets for Patrick."

Thomas shook his head. His shoulders slumped, and he looked exhausted. "No. We were hot and heavy for a while; then three days ago, she tells me she's in love with another guy."

Oh, that poor man. I hadn't been much better, though I would never have broken up with him. (Well, maybe I would have. Tongue wrestling with Dylan technically counted as cheating on Thomas, and I'd had every intention of sleeping with Dylan right there on the floor of the bathroom at the funeral home.) Anyway, I'd wanted the stability Thomas offered. The fact that he liked to discuss the state of our relationship had been a bonus I now missed. I wondered if he could run Dylan through a brief tutorial…

"I'm so sorry," I said. "She's an idiot. You're the perfect man."

Some of his tiredness dropped away, and he laughed. "Lacey—God, I miss you sometimes. You're the only woman I've ever met who wanted so badly to fall in love with me. You tried so hard."

Heat rose up my neck. I had tried.

"How are things going with you and Dylan? I noticed a few media flaps recently."

It was my turn to laugh. "How very nice of you not to come right out and ask why I've lied about Dylan to the media."

He lifted one shoulder, but this time it came off as rakish and urbane. "You're welcome."

I didn't want to say too much. Some things were between Dylan and me, and they needed to remain that way. "We hit a rough patch. We broke up for a little while, and now we're in negotiations to get back together."

"You're in negotiations?"

It was my turn for the debonair shrug. "I'm not into rushing. It triggers some bad habits I'd rather keep in my past."

"Good for you," he said.

Luma kicked me under the table, which was her way of telling me that having an intimate tête-à-tête with Thomas wasn't working for her. Besides, I needed to schmooze Steve and Patrick. They hadn't met Luma before.

Patrick smiled in my direction. I think he knew Luma had kicked me. "Lacey, I think it's awesome that you're branching out and representing other acts."

I didn't mention that I'd lost KMG. Though I hadn't admitted it yet, being fired had hurt. Now that my relationship with Dylan was being remodeled and my friendships with Levi and Gavin had been rekindled, I had time to think about what I'd lost. I couldn't separate the business and personal aspects because KMG had been my family.

"Thanks. Luma, Jane, and I formed LJL Talent Management. We signed Something Wicked, the next band up, a few months ago." Plug, plug, plug. "They're a quartet, all girls, with some powerful songs. We're going to have them cut a few demos when we get back home."

Luma joined in, and together, we pimped our newest discovery. Neither of us mentioned More Than Swagger. I knew Luma wanted to, but I warned her about trying to sell more than one band at a time. Steve needed to know we believed in Something Wicked, not that we were hedging our bets by throwing darts at a bunch of bands to see what stuck where. That wasn't our business plan.

Plus, I wasn't getting along too well with Bennett. Every time I saw him, I had to take him to task over something — usually alcohol related — and I didn't want to manage a band I had to babysit like that. I'd resolved to tell Jane and Luma that I was finished with them, and if they wanted to continue representing MTS, I wasn't going to be a part of it. But I waffled because I liked the rest of the guys. If they fired Bennett, I was sure they could become something remarkable. In the meantime, I had big plans for Something Wicked.

Before long, I drew Patrick and Steve into the conversation. I didn't want to do a hard sell, not before they'd seen the band and expressed an interest in their music, so our discussion wandered over many topics. After a few rounds of drinks, Something Wicked played. We abandoned our table and moved into the crowd on the floor. Thomas stood behind me, his body inches from mine because the venue was decently packed. Whenever one of us moved, body parts came into contact. As Luma was plastered to my side, and Patrick and Steve were also within touchy-feely distance, it wasn't a big deal — until he snaked an arm around my waist and pulled me to him.

His goatee brushed my ear. "Lacey, do me a huge favor?"

I tilted my face back. His tone held a note of panic I'd never heard from him before. "Sure. What's wrong?"

"My ex is here. She's about ten feet to my left, and the last time I looked over, she was staring at me."

Since I was aimed in that direction anyway, I let my gaze slide over the crowd. Sure enough, a woman was watching us. She was one of those tall, cool women with candy-apple red lipstick that made men think of blowjobs. "Blond? Black strappy dress? Fuck-me lipstick?"

"Yes."

"Damn, Thomas. She's hot. I'd do her." The guy with her wasn't bad-looking either, but I thought Thomas had him beat.

He squeezed me tighter, unintentionally. I think. "Geez, Lacey. Thank you for that image. I will treasure it forever."

"No problem. I owe you."

"Pretend you're with me, and you can consider your debt paid in full."

That request made me uncomfortable. If Dylan found out, he wouldn't be happy. While we technically weren't together, we were together…if that makes any sense.

"Okay, but no kissing or fondling."

"Noted. I'm not into PDA anyway. We'll keep it classy."

I trusted him to do that. Besides, he didn't say it, but I figured the blonde was the one he wanted to be kissing and fondling. "What's her name?"

"Justine."

While Something Wicked played, Thomas kept his arm around me. Sometimes he altered his position by putting his hands on my hips, but he didn't make me uncomfortable.

Luma leaned in at one point. "What the hell are you doing?"

I'd shared the details of my last date with Dylan, as well as the fact that we'd had post-breakup sex. "Thomas's ex-girlfriend, who shattered his heart, is over there with her latest boy toy."

"So, now you're being a girl toy? I don't like this, Lacey. You said you wanted to get back with Dylan."

She was genuinely pissed about my behavior.

I grabbed her sleeve when she went to put distance between us, and I hauled her closer. "It's nothing. Thomas is being a gentleman, and I trust him not to try anything. There's no harm done in letting him keep his arm around me. You'd do the same for Gavin. Or Levi."

I played a hunch with that last part. I'd caught Luma checking out those guys every now and again. When I called her on it, she'd shrug and say anybody who wasn't looking at them wasn't into men, which she was.

"Or Dylan," she hissed. "But you'd be the bitch across the room glaring at me for fucking around with your ex."

And I'd know they were faking it. "Luma, be nice. Thomas was good to me."

"If Dylan was at a bar right now with his arm around a pretty girl, what would you think?"

A pang went through me, though I knew Dylan hadn't looked at another woman since the moment he'd first set eyes on me. She was right, but I didn't know how to get out of my agreement with Thomas. "Want to switch places?" Let's see if she had a better idea.

Luma lifted a brow. "Yes."

Without consulting Thomas, we switched places. Facing him, Luma wrapped her arms around his neck and drew him down to her. The open-mouthed kiss she laid on him had my jaw dropping. Thomas didn't resist, but he didn't participate—at first. A few seconds passed, and he lifted Luma against him. He held her with one hand on her ass. The other tangled in her long, dark tresses.

Just when I thought they might come up for air, Luma wrapped her legs around Thomas's waist. He kneaded her ass, pressing her intimately against his man parts. I risked a glance at Patrick and found him watching with a stunned expression on his face, which I assume mirrored mine.

Justine pushed through the crowd, but Thomas was already stumbling away with Luma still attached to his body. Acting quickly, I intercepted the woman. She was here with another man. She had no right to interfere with whatever was going on with Thomas and Luma.

"Hi," I said. "I hope you aren't planning to go after them."

They'd disappeared through the door to the lobby. Whether they wanted a quickie or they were just acting really fucking well was no business of mine.

She hissed out a stream of air. "He's here with you?"

I shrugged. "Now he's here with her." Sidling closer, I traced my fingertip down one of her long blond locks. "You lost your chance. Thomas is one man in a million, and you blew it. Turn around and go back. That man you came with isn't looking too happy right now. Don't blow it with that one. You're not getting any younger."

She huffed and puffed, but she eventually went back to her current meal ticket. Maybe she'd found out he wasn't as well-heeled as Thomas. Whatever. Her loss. I stared at the entrance, wondering what had happened with Thomas and Luma. I'd never seen him look at her in a way that would indicate interest.

Returning to Patrick and Steve, I rocked out to Something Wicked. A new sense of freedom filled me. I'd done a good thing tonight, very possibly for two of my friends.

Patrick leaned down to me. "What was that?"

"Thomas getting over Justine, I hope." And perhaps Luma ending her dry spell.

"I've never seen Thomas like that before."

In my pocket, my phone buzzed with a text from Luma. *Don't wait up. Will call you in the morning.*

That answered that question. I grinned at Patrick. "Then it's about time."

He matched my grin with one of his own. "Yes, it is."

Chapter Ten

Steve asked me to send him a copy of the demo once we had it. I wasn't sure if he was impressed with Something Wicked—who had a truly wicked tour that netted them many new fans—or thankful that Thomas was out of his depression.

I needed to get that demo cut. Their web site was getting a lot of hits. I updated it to include information on what was coming soon, and I had Luma make sure their social media pages were active and attractive.

I was dying to ask Luma what had happened, but I was also afraid to know. I mean, I hadn't slept with Thomas—and I didn't want to—but it was weird that one of my best friends most likely had. And what did it mean? Were they seeing each other now, or had it been a one-night stand?

It's not like I could talk about this with Dylan. Thomas had always been a topic we avoided discussing. I don't think Dylan bore any ill will toward Thomas, but if I suddenly started wondering about the man's sex life, he was bound to take it as jealousy.

Which I wasn't. Not really.

Okay, maybe I was a little jealous. My relationship with Thomas had been linear and uncomplicated. I missed that.

I called Dylan when I got back, but between his schedule and mine, we couldn't settle on plans for a second date until the next weekend. Though we snatched short conversations on the phone and exchanged texts, I wasn't able to free a night until after Something Wicked had recorded their demo. Once they did, I sent it off to Steve. The other guy hadn't shown up at the date we played near Philadelphia, so it turned out Steve was the only one biting. (Unless you count Thomas and the big hickey he'd left on Luma's shoulder.)

Luma, Jane, and I met for an early dinner on the day of my second date with Dylan.

I started our meeting bluntly. "If More Than Swagger doesn't kill it at Lollapalooza, I'm finished with them. I barely have time to shave my legs. I do not have time to devote to a crappy band who can't bother to put in the time and effort required to learn the few songs they've written. Plus, people who deal with us need to know we have a quality product, that when we represent a band, they have talent, drive, and a work ethic."

This came because none of us had been able to confirm that More Than Swagger was practicing at all. When I'd asked Charlotte, she'd blushed and shrugged, and I'd felt like an ass for asking her to inform on her brother.

Luma slurped the last of her cola through her straw. "I concur. I talked to Leo last night. He's not sure the band is going to stay together. Bennett isn't showing up to practices, and he's blowing them off when they call or stop by his place."

I knew Bennett was the loose cannon. I'd tried so hard to like him, but part of me blamed him for Dylan walking out on me in Grand Rapids. I was still steamed about that. Yes, I'd told him to go, but he'd left me to get a cab home. The dickhead was comfortable sending me to drive halfway across the state with a stranger.

That was definitely something we needed to discuss before we moved too far forward.

"All right," Jane said. "How sure are we that our relationship is winding down?"

"Sure enough that I want you to have paperwork ready," Luma said. "This sucks. I really liked them."

I put my hand over hers like I was going to deliver some pithy words of wisdom, but my unpredictable mouth got the better of me. I didn't lie, so don't worry yourself that I relapsed. (Spoiler: To date,

I haven't, except for little white lies. And even John said that kind of lying every once in a while is normal.)

"Luma, I really want to know how much you *liked* Thomas while we were in Boston."

Jane gasped. She smacked Luma's arm. She tried the same thing with me, but I moved out of reach. "What the hell happened in Boston, and why am I just now hearing about this? You've been back for five days. This is bullshit. Dish. Now."

We'd been busy. I shot Jane an apologetic wince. "Sorry. I wanted to tell you, but I don't know the details. The last I saw, Luma was wrapped around Thomas, and he was carrying her out of the bar. Then she texted me that she was staying the night with him."

Luma knew her time of silence had come to an abrupt end. "Are you sure you want to know, Lacey?"

"No. I mean, yes. I want to know."

Jane suddenly reconsidered. "Wait. Lacey, this is kind of weird. We've never hooked up with each other's exes before. It seems almost incestuous."

It was weird, but not in a bad way. I thought after a few initial awkward moments, I'd get over it. "Thomas is a great guy. Luma deserves someone wonderful. I can deal."

Luma looked relieved. "Good. Because he was like John Legend, smooth and sensual. He knew when to go slow and low, and when to kick it up a notch. And he was a stallion, ladies. He rode me all night long. When Lacey picked me up the next morning, I hadn't been asleep yet."

Come to think of it, she had been tired when I'd picked her up. She'd crashed until we got to Philly. Except the obvious, there wasn't much I could say. "Wow."

Jane gaped at Luma. We'd been privy to details before, many more than this, but this was the first time Luma hadn't attributed her lover's stamina to his skin color. "So, it looks like you've had black and now you've gone back."

Luma shrugged. "For now. We're not looking to get all serious or anything, but the sex was awesome, so he's coming in this weekend to hang out with me."

No wonder she'd made an effort to keep our schedule clear. And I'd thought it was because I'd complained about not having a night free to see Dylan. I guess I can be a little self-centered at times. "You weren't going to tell us?"

"I wasn't going to tell *you*," she said. "I wanted to see if it was just a one-off thing or if it's more before I said anything. Plus, I didn't know how you'd take it. You've been doing so well with not washing your hands or lying that I didn't want to set you off again."

How sweet and thoughtful. "You don't have to worry about me. I'm doing okay. It feels different this time, like the part of me that fed those urges has shriveled up and been replaced with…peace. I feel normal, and I can't remember ever feeling this way before. Am I jealous about you and Thomas? A little, but only because Dylan and I aren't having an easy time of it. Mostly I'm happy for you. If you want him for one night or forever, I'm happy for you."

By the time I got done rambling, both Jane and Luma's eyes shone bright with unshed tears. I stared at the pair of them, wondering why they were looking at me like that, and then I realized what I'd said. I'd leaped a huge mental hurdle. Now all I had to do was put my relationship with Dylan on solid footing.

The server chose that moment to deliver our food. Once everything was situated, I dug into my salad. "Now that I'm finished stealing Luma's moment, I want to hear every single detail. It's time to brag."

"Yeah," Jane said. "Did he have a great breast stroke?"

"Oh, man," Luma said, glowing with glee. "He was the best I ever had."

Just after Luma finished her story, which did take a while, Leo called in a panic. More Than Swagger had a crisis only I could handle, or at least it seemed so at the time. After lunch, Jane had to get back to the office. She was a week from taking her bar exam, and her study schedule was crazy. We were all looking forward to Lollapalooza because it would be a vacation from our day jobs.

I wanted nothing more than to get home and prep for my date, but Luma had to take her father to a doctor's appointment. She didn't have another job, so by rights, she should have been the one to field this MTS issue, but her mother was visiting her aunt in Texas, and Luma's father had a seizure disorder and couldn't drive.

So, I agreed to go see the band and called Dylan to postpone our date. He wasn't having any of it.

"This can wait until tomorrow," he told me.

"I'd rather not wait. I don't want to have this hanging over me." It was a dark raincloud that would ruin my night. "I want to be able to focus on you and nothing else."

On the other end, I heard him sigh. "How about I pick you up, we swing by and put out this fire, and then the rest of the night is ours?"

I liked his plan, but I was leery about having him anywhere near More Than Swagger. I wanted to spend time with him, so I swallowed my trepidation. "Okay. Pick me up in fifteen minutes."

This wouldn't be one of those dates where I tried on twelve outfits and spent a lot of time with my makeup. Dylan wanted to take me to a park where they were going to project a movie onto a large screen. People would sit on blankets and watch. I dressed in jeans and a cute baby tee, and I grabbed a sweatshirt in case the temperature dropped.

The sum total of my makeup consisted of mascara and cherry lip gloss.

Mostly I looked forward to spooning on a blanket with Dylan. He'd keep up a running commentary on the movie, peppering funny or ironic statements for my pleasure. I loved when he repeated dramatic lines in a sexy and suggestive way, which almost always led to kissing and groping.

The knock on my door came five minutes after I got home. I greeted him with a kiss on the cheek. His manner was a bit prickly. He didn't return my kiss or try for something more satisfying. "Are you ready?"

"Not quite. Did you bring mosquito spray?"

"It'll be fine."

I headed to the hall closet upstairs where I thought I had some squirreled in the back. "You say that until you're cranky because you're itching."

He didn't come up with me, and when I came back down, I found him wandering in the kitchen, opening and closing cupboards. That wasn't something a man should do on a second date.

"Can I help you find something?"

"Nope. Just looking at how you've set everything up. I would have put the glasses by the sink and the plates near the stove."

The kitchen was a good deal larger than the one at my previous place, and some of the cupboards were empty. I knew he was thinking about what he'd change when he moved in. That brought me to a serious crossroads. The fact that he took what he wanted figured heavily in the problems we were having.

I didn't want to fight, not tonight. More than anything, I just wanted to be with him. I yearned for the easy camaraderie of our early friendship, when it had been uncomplicated by heartache, lies, and unmet expectations.

"I'm ready to go. Do you have a blanket?"

"Yes. I have everything covered, except the bug spray, and you've seen to that. Let's go."

He drove. I directed him to the house that had the garage where Something Wicked and More Than Swagger practiced. Though I really would have preferred for him to wait in the car, he followed me inside.

"How long do you think it'll take?"

"I hope not long." Part of me wanted to share the fact that I was nearly finished with this band, but Dylan wasn't my boyfriend, and he wasn't a colleague. I couldn't justify sharing that kind of information — especially when LJL hadn't made a final decision — with anybody outside the company.

Leo and Bastien met us in the driveway. They were shooting hoops. Leo sank a three-pointer as we approached. He did a double take when he saw that Dylan was with me.

"Hey, Lacey. Thanks for coming."

Bastien, who had caught the ball on the bounce, said, "Yeah. It's pretty bad."

"What's pretty bad? You guys didn't give very many details on the phone."

Dylan peered at me closely, his eyes narrowed. "You pushed back our date and rushed over here without getting the details?"

I wanted to *shush* him, but I settled for ignoring him. Jane had taken the call. She was the one who'd insisted they needed me to be here. In retrospect, yes, I should have asked for details. However, I wasn't going to throw my business partner and best friend under the bus for any reason. For starters, she'd never left me stranded in Grand Rapids.

Leo grimaced. "Bennett showed up for practice late. He's drunk, and he won't help with the arrangement on the song you told us to redo. It's kind of hard to do that without a drummer."

Jane had warned them that if they didn't practice and improve, we wouldn't be able to continue representing them. I understood their panic, but never again would I interrupt my evening with this kind of stuff. It wasn't like they were bringing us any sort of profit yet. Something Wicked was just beginning to pay out, and that money was a trickle. They barely covered expenses. Ideally we would have a band like Kiss Me Goodnight to help us float the cost of developing new talent, but we didn't. Representing these two bands was a full-time job, and two of us had full-time jobs on top of that.

I wasn't complaining—well, yeah, I was. I was pissed that I'd been called here to deal with this crap. Waves of Dylan's fury washed over me, and that didn't help. I mean, I'd been looking forward to spending some more time getting to know the man I loved, and now that I was here to handle this "emergency," it seemed like a waste of time. If the situation was so bad, why were Leo and Bastien out here shooting hoops? I knew Dylan was thinking the same thing. He was right. He'd been right all along, and at times like this, I hated when he was right.

Inside the garage, chaos reigned. Ari and Max prowled the converted space. They followed Bennett as he wandered around the room with a can of beer in his hand, bitching about Luma, Jane, and me. Especially me.

"She's so full of herself. Oh, look how she bats her eyes so prettily while she doesn't do shit for you and takes all of your money."

Their take of the Grand Rapids date and of the two we'd been able to secure for them afterward hadn't been much. Expenses were paid from their percentage of the profits. After travel and lodging, there wasn't much left. When KMG had first started out, they were happy to have fifty bucks to invest back into the band's expenses.

Not for the first time, I ripped into Bennett. "You aren't popular enough to make money. I'm still begging venues to take you. The last show you did was for free."

"That's bullshit," Bennett said, whirling to face me without even the decency to seem embarrassed.

I was struck by the difference in his demeanor when he was rip-roaring drunk. He'd moved way past flirty, and now he was downright belligerent. He stumbled closer and scowled in my face.

"It's not bullshit," Dylan said. He shoved Bennett back, putting another foot between me and the drunk jerk. "It's the business. You have to do this because you love it, not for the money."

"Says the dickwad who's fucking his band's manager. Is that a bonus you give out to everybody?" He leered, and I was glad we weren't alone. Bennett hadn't behaved in a threatening manner before, but now he scared me. Hatred burned behind his eyes. "I'll take some of that."

Dylan wrapped his hand around my upper arm. "We're leaving, Lacey."

Afraid or not, I had to have the last word. I wished Dylan hadn't witnessed this. Although without him, I probably would've wasted more time trying to explain the way things worked or calming Bennett down. That was one positive effect of Dylan's presence, but the negative ones were forthcoming.

"Leo, Max, you need to evaluate why you're in a band. Figure out where you see this going and if what you're doing and allowing to happen will get you there. Jane was clear about our expectations. I never want to get a call like this again, and I'm not dealing with Bennett when he's drunk. You've wasted my time, and I don't appreciate it."

Dylan dragged me to the car, making an unnecessarily big production of it. I didn't appreciate being treated like meat, but I waited until we got into the car before I said anything.

"Don't ever do that again."

"I was trying to help. There was no reason for you to be there. It's not your job to deal with a drunken asshole."

Underage drunken asshole that I represent. "Yes, it is. And that's not what I meant. I know you were trying to help us get out of there faster, but dragging me out like I'm some kind of errant child isn't going to win you brownie points with me."

"Lacey, this was a bullshit waste of our time. We're late for the movie. We probably won't get a good spot now. I had a perfect evening planned, and you let them ruin it. That Bennett is a grade-A asshole, but you seem to like him."

I couldn't think of any part of today's interaction that would give him the impression that I liked Bennett, and Dylan's attitude was pissing me off even more. "When you left me in Grand Rapids, he's the one who came back and made sure I got home."

Dylan hit the steering wheel and slammed on the brakes. We were at a stop sign, but it was an angry stop. "Here it is. Now you're going to throw that in my face."

"I hadn't planned to. Yes, it's something we need to discuss, but in the context of a larger problem." I didn't want to talk about those things tonight, especially given Dylan's PMS mood. There was no way he'd be reasonable right now. "I understand that you're upset about the interruption. I'm not happy about it either, but treating me like that was wrong."

He dismissed me with an arrogant flip of his hand. "You needed to leave. I made sure it happened."

He was missing the point. I hissed/grunted through my nose. It sounded growlish, but it wasn't. "You're not the boss of me! You don't get to decide when I'm finished with a conversation or a client."

"You would've been there all night, trying to deal with that asswipe. He has the hots for you. He's just doing this shit to get your attention, and I think you like it."

I stared at him, equal parts hurt and angry, in complete silence.

Doing his best to ignore my glare, he kept driving. Finally, he growled, "What?"

"You think I like having to deal with immature boys playing at being in a band?"

Unwilling to backtrack, he shrugged. "Seems that way. Seems like you're willing to spend time with anybody but me."

"We don't live together anymore, and I don't represent your band. That cuts out about eighty percent of the time we spent together. I have a new business, and that takes more of my time. You were supportive of it when I started, and you've admitted that you were wrong to not have supported me when I needed you to."

"When you started, I told you that you'd need to quit working for Hanover."

"Well, I kind of need the income." Oh, I got an A in sarcasm for my tone. "This venture has yet to pay out, and I no longer have income coming from Kiss Me Goodnight."

He fumed for a bit, most likely swallowing back comments on how I deserved it because of what I'd done. "I don't like it, Lacey. I want you to quit. I'll talk to Daisy. I'll get you KMG back. We can't agree on a new manager, so we're twisting in the wind right now."

"You want me to quit because you're jealous?"

"They're not worth your time. Bennett is dangerous. He's one tequila worm away from jail. You know, I used to come first with you. There was a time when you'd drop everything to be with me. There was a time when I meant something to you."

Had he morphed into an oversized child when I wasn't looking? "Dylan, don't be an ass. It's not like I'm your girlfriend."

He signaled left when he should have gone right.

"Where are you taking me?"

"Home." He pressed his lips together, which highlighted their sensual nature—not that I was enjoying it at the moment—and flared his nostrils. "Not my home, your home. It was supposed to be *our* home, but that's not what happened, is it?"

He jerked the wheel right and pulled to the shoulder, bringing the car to a halt. He threw it in park and turned the full force of his glare at me. I've told you before that I don't find Dylan sexy when he's furious. That's still true.

"Not my girlfriend? *Not* my girlfriend? What the hell are you, then, Lacey? What the fuck did you think we were doing?" he shouted. Less than a foot from my face, his voice roared through my consciousness and activated a healthy dose of my own anger.

"I don't know what we're doing. That's part of our problem, and it's always been that way. I *never* know what's going on. You decide things without telling me. You decided we should live together, so you moved in. Twice. You decided we were over, so you left me—on the other side of the state. Now I'm supposed to be your girlfriend? Since when? When did you ask me? Or is this another thing you decided for me?"

Instead of responding, he threw the car in gear, churned gravel, and took me home. We made it in record time. He stopped in front of my door, and he sat there in front of the steering wheel, his chest heaving in anger. "Tonight isn't happening."

"It's good you decided that. Thanks for telling me."

I pulled the latch to open the door, and he grabbed my wrist. "Lacey—"

"No, Dylan. Don't say anything else. I can't do this. Not anymore. I'm tired of fighting with you." I chewed up the words and spat them at him, and they were the truth. I got out of the car and stalked up the steps and into *my* apartment. I slammed the door without looking behind me and leaned against it heavily.

It felt good to get the truth out—so fucking good. A weight had vanished, like it used to do when I lied, but what took its place was worse. If this was my reward, then why did it ache so fucking badly? I rubbed the center of my chest as the tides of misery washed over me.

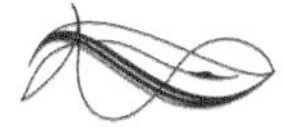

I neither saw nor talked to Dylan for three weeks. I wondered if he was pouting or if he'd given up on me. Thinking about him was exhausting. It used to energize me, and that change made me inordinately sad. After the first week, my depression turned to anger. How dare he treat me like this? I thought I'd been clear about what I wanted and how fast or slow I wanted to take things. I didn't think I'd been unreasonable.

Levi did his duty and informed me that Dylan's writer's block had cleared up with a vengeance. He was cranking out new songs and revising them faster than the band could write music. "They're all angry and sad," he'd said. "Most of them aren't really our sound. They're good songs, but they don't fit KMG."

When I took Monty to lunch, he started the conversation with, "So, you and Uncle Dylan had another fight? Fantastic. That's not going to get a ring on your finger anytime soon."

I'd replied that I wasn't looking for a ring, but I was really thinking Dylan would probably marry me without telling me about it. One day I'd look down and wonder why I was wearing a wedding ring, and then shit would hit the fan. Monty said Dylan was either locked in his room or the practice studio, and whenever anybody tried to talk to him, he bit their head off.

The third week, my passive-aggressive side came out. I was going to make Dylan regret losing me if I had to kill him in the process.

We all ended up in the same hall of the same hotel for Lollapalooza. That wasn't coincidence. I'd booked the rooms in a block back when I represented all three bands. Two of the rooms belonged to Kiss Me Goodnight, one went to Something Wicked, another went to More Than Swagger — I didn't care if they had to sleep three to a bed — and the last belonged to Jane, Luma, and me.

It made for some awkward moments. When we first arrived, More Than Swagger was already there. I'd forced them to make their own travel arrangements because I was tired of listening to Bennett's bitching. My opinion of him had gone from bad to worse. Every interaction was increasingly negative, and I wasn't ashamed to admit that he made me extremely uneasy. He had a drinking problem, and he was taking his band down with him. If they let him, they deserved what they got.

I seriously regretted not dropping them before this event, and I didn't want them in any way associated with LJL. Luma had come to my side, but Jane wanted to wait until after the concert. She wanted to give them one more chance, and I knew she needed to be burned by them in a big way before she gave up. This was quintessential Jane. She often puts too much time and effort into those who don't deserve it.

I don't count myself in that number. I'm totally worth it.

Nevertheless, when we got there, I went down to the boys' room to check on them. Leo answered my knock. "Hey, Lacey. Come on in. We were just going through one of the arrangements."

Ari, Max, and Bastien smiled at me. They were excited to be here, to have this opportunity.

Bennett sneered at me, but he addressed Max. "They sent the bitch. Told you we're screwed."

Ari cleared his throat. "Knock it off, Bennett."

"And stop drinking," I added. "You can barely play sober, and you're wasted already."

He lifted a can of beer in my direction. "I'm not even buzzed. You know how I can tell? Because you're not fuckable yet."

"Enough." Max and Bastien said it together, both rising to their feet. "Lacey, we'll take care of this. He'll be sober by morning."

Bennett cracked open the can. Bastien took it from him and poured it down the sink. Ari and Max confiscated the rest of his stash.

Though I eyed the drama with detachment, I was glad I wasn't alone with Bennett and that pretty soon, this would no longer be my problem. "Good luck," I said as bade them goodbye.

On the way back to my room, where I'd left Jane and Luma unpacking, I passed Daisy and Dylan in the hall.

Daisy lifted her chin in my direction. I'd only seen her from a distance since she'd fired me. She hadn't since said a word directly to me, and that didn't change now. But it was a sort-of greeting. I smiled in response, and she softened a little. I realized she'd probably been avoiding me because she knew she'd give in and forgive me if only we talked. I put that on my list of things to accomplish while I was here.

Dylan glared at me, not bothering to temper his expression because we were in public. (Yes, there were other people in the hall.) He needed to watch out. Somebody (like me) might snap a picture, merge it with a grumpy kitty meme, and post it on the band's Facebook page. They hadn't changed the password, which is the first thing I would have done if I'd fired somebody with access.

After the descriptions of his moody behavior I'd heard from Monty and Levi (Gavin had opted to discuss anything *but* Dylan), my impish nature got the better of me. I winked. He seriously needed to lighten up. The man needed to get laid. Lack of sex made him downright morose. When he passed me, I slapped his ass. He turned, probably meaning to glare harder, but the look of surprise on his face ruined that attempt. I blew him a kiss. Maybe I would pretend we were back together, that I'd decided without discussing it with him. See how he liked it.

Cuz I kind of did.

Monty and I had a date later that afternoon. He wanted to see Arctic Monkeys perform on the second stage, and so did I. When I knocked on the door of Daisy's room to pick him up, Dylan answered. He stared at me for the longest time, like he was wondering if he'd been drugged and taken to Fantasy Island. I teased him by running my tongue along the edge of my upper lip, tasting my cherry lip gloss.

"Old Man, is that my date?" Monty appeared at Dylan's side. Now that they were next to one another, the growing and filling out Monty had done lately made him look even more like Dylan's kid.

"You're too young to date," Dylan said. His voice came out quiet, though I think he'd tried for dry.

Monty grinned, sidled past his uncle, and offered me his arm. "Ready, Aunt Lacey?"

I linked my arm through his.

Dylan scowled. "She's not your aunt."

Before I could say anything to defuse his temper (or maybe set him off even more), Monty laughed. "Just because you're taking your sweet-ass time sealing the deal doesn't mean I have to wait."

Dylan's scowl grew deeper. I patted his cheek. "You look like a sourpuss when you do that. Relax and bring sexy back."

Surprise softened his expression and made his eyes sparkle. He did look damned attractive.

Monty and I giggled all the way to the elevator. Inside, he spread out against the back wall, taking up more space than a gangly teen should. "He's got it bad. I was looking at his song notebook, and he's basically writing love letters to you. Want me to steal it so you can see?"

Dylan's notebook was sacred, a place where nobody but him could tread. I'd moved it to clean, but I'd never once opened it.

"You shouldn't be looking at his private stuff. Leave it alone. If he finds you with it, you'll be in real trouble."

He shrugged. "Then he shouldn't leave it in the drawer with the T-shirts I like to wear."

It took me a moment to realize Monty was wearing Dylan's clothes. Dylan was possessive of some of his things. I'd known which shirts he didn't mind me wearing and which to avoid. Monty had chosen an off-limits vintage Skinny Puppy shirt, so it seemed he didn't share my respect for boundaries. It must be a family trait.

Hanging out with Monty was fun. We saw Arctic Monkeys, and I kept him out for MS MR. When we got back, the door to the room was propped open. This was happening up and down the hallway. People came and went, and the entire floor was like one big party. Daisy had her press packet for the festival in her hands. She smacked it onto the tiny round-top table under the window. "I swear Lacey said we were supposed to be on the main stage."

Seated at the chair next to the table, Audra looked up from her tablet. Daisy in a snit looked a lot like Dylan in a snit, only more feminine, and not because Daisy was wearing hot pink and black. I didn't envy Audra having to live in a house with three Days.

Like I tried to do when Dylan went off on something, Audra appeared unimpressed. "If she was still your manager, you could ask her."

Daisy's lips pressed together, and she parked her fist on her hip.

I chose this moment to announce our presence. "Hi. We're back. I didn't feed Monty, but he's getting cranky, so I know he's hungry."

Daisy stared at me like a bug who dared invade her shower. Before she could decide between screaming for help or squishing the life out of me, Audra got up and came over. "Thanks for taking him. We have so much to do tonight to get ready for tomorrow." She grabbed her purse. "Come on, Monty. Let's get some takeout for your mother. She could use something to eat as well."

The cowardly version of me would have crept out of the room with Audra and Monty, but I must have left her at home. I came inside. "I was still working out the details when I stopped representing your band. None of that was finalized. I confirmed Kiss Me Goodnight last month when I confirmed my other bands, but I didn't ask for details. It was no longer my business to know what was going on with you guys."

The wind left her sails. "This is my fault."

"No," I said. "It's mine. I'm sorry, Daisy. I'm sorry for the things I said about you." I'd already apologized to everybody else. "I had no right to drag you into the drama between Dylan and me."

Daisy sank down on the end of one of the queen beds. She patted the spot next to her, and I obeyed her silent command.

"When I got over being furious with you, I was mad that you would say such horrible things about us. I mean, you were family. We loved you. I loved you like the sister I never had."

Betrayal hurts. That's why it's one of the worst things you can do to a person you love. I still feel bad about the heartache I'd caused.

Daisy squeezed my hand. "When Dylan told me about what happened to you when you were a kid, I thought it was just another lie you'd told. Then Monty came home and said he'd talked to you about it. I was pissed that you would lie to him, but then he looked it up on the Internet. There were no pictures of you, but there were pictures of your father, stepmother, and brother."

I resemble my father. It isn't something I like to advertise, but he was a handsome man. The ugliness was all on the inside.

"I'm sorry that happened to you."

I shrugged. "But you were right anyway. I needed to get over it. I let that one day control my life for almost twenty years. I used my behaviors as a defense to drive people away when they got too close. It was effective. I'm sorry, Daisy. I've come a long way since the last time we talked. I wish we could one day be friends again. I miss you."

Levi came to the door. "Daisy, we're going out to grab some food. Oh, hey, Lacey. Do you want to get some dinner with us?"

I got to my feet and sloughed off the embarrassment of my mushy admission. "No, but thanks. Jane, Luma, and I have plans with Something Wicked and More Than Swagger."

Gavin came inside, as did Dylan. He wore his firm expression, which I found infinitely more attractive than many of the others he'd donned lately. A flame sparked deep in his eyes as he regarded me. "That guy puts his hands on you, and I will break his fingers. It's awfully hard to drum with broken fingers."

"Yep." Daisy stood with the rest of us. "I can attest to that."

We all looked at Dylan with various degrees of scolding in our expressions.

He returned the favor by frowning at us all like we were idiots. "It wasn't my fault. She punched a wall, and not because of me."

I heard Luma and Jane coming down the hall. That was my cue to leave. As I went past Dylan, I said, "Only I get to say who puts his hands on me." I didn't stick around to see his reaction.

As it happened, Bennett didn't show up for dinner. He'd hooked up with friends and was nowhere to be found. I was glad for that. His negative energy and sour disposition cast dark shadows I didn't need in my life. I wanted to eat in peace and celebrate this momentous occasion.

Jane pulled Violet aside, and when they returned to our table, Violet said, "I'll fill in for you guys, but I'm warning you now that I don't really know your songs."

"That's okay," Leo said, though he looked anything but all right with it. "Neither does Bennett."

I felt bad for them, but not too bad. They'd known for some time that Bennett wasn't cutting it, and they'd let him stay part of the band. This was the grave they'd dug, and now they had to lie in it. I didn't comment.

More Than Swagger excused themselves early, taking Violet with them to do a few run-throughs. India, Bree, and Charlotte stayed with us. We caught the last three shows on the main stage and didn't get back to the hotel until after midnight.

As we'd spent half the day traveling — it had taken as long to get into the city as it had taken to drive from Detroit to the outer limits of Chicago — we were tired. Jane called the first shower. Luma and I brushed our teeth and vegged on the bed as we waited for our turns.

The knock on the door didn't surprise us. People had been going up and down the halls crashing into things. I didn't expect to sleep in silence tonight. The knock came again, so I dragged myself over to see if somebody was really there.

Dylan was on the other side of the peephole. He'd propped his weight on the hand that rested against the wall next to our door. I couldn't tell much about his face because of the curved glass distorting his image, but I could see the day's growth of stubble darkening his cheeks. Damn, he looked good.

He knocked a third time, and I opened the door. I was wearing a shirt and panties, but he'd seen me in less. "Can I help you?"

His gaze started at my feet and moved up my body, a blatant caress that made me tingle. Then he shoved me into the room, slammed the door shut behind him, and pinned me to the wall separating the small entryway from the bathroom.

Without a word, he devoured me. This was my Dylan — taking what he wanted. His lips skimmed my cheeks and eyes before returning to possess my lips. I loved the way he cupped my head, holding me still and tilting it to access the areas he most wanted to taste. Then he cradled one hand against my nape and filled the other with half of my ass. He lifted me against him, grinding his man parts into me. I never wanted this to stop.

"I'm tired of fighting with you." He spoke in a low tone as he nibbled at my lower lip. From the flavor of alcohol on his breath, I deduced he had been drinking. "I'm tired of being apart. This isn't what I want. Is this the way you want us to be?"

The bathroom door opened. "Hi, Dylan." Jane came out, thankfully wearing more than a towel. "Conjugal visit?"

He lifted his head and stared at her, blinking several times as if to clear his vision.

"She's real," I said. "Luma's here too."

"You're not alone?"

Luma, toiletry bag in hand, threw a smile at Dylan before disappearing into the bathroom. Bitch. The next shower was supposed to be mine.

"No. Not alone."

He stumbled into the main part of the room, where Jane was crawling into one of the queen beds, and he fell into the other. I turned him over. His eyes were closed, and he didn't resist me.

"He pass out?" Jane asked as she squirted moisturizer on her hands.

"Yep."

"Looks like Luma's sleeping with me tonight."

I got Dylan's shoes off, but I left his shirt and jeans alone. I was tempted to unbutton his pants, but he'd probably freak if he woke up in a roomful of women with his fly open. Because he was on top of the comforter, I took an extra blanket from the closet and covered him. Then I showered and climbed into bed next to him. Ten bucks said I'd wake up in his arms.

Chapter Eleven

Did you bet against me? Because I might owe you some cash.

When I woke up, Dylan was in exactly the same position. I put my ear on his chest to see if his heart was beating, and I jumped when his hand flopped onto my head. Looking up, I caught his mouth stretching with the beginning of a sleepy smile. He didn't open his eyes, though.

"Want us to leave you two alone?" Light from the bathroom shone behind Luma. Their bed was empty, so I figured Jane was in the bathroom. My guess was confirmed when the light source abruptly vanished.

I glanced at the clock. It was ten thirty. We needed to eat and get Something Wicked set up for their one o'clock performance. "No. We need to get going."

Dylan groaned. "Back to bed, Lacey. Worthwhile."

"Stay in bed with a hung-over man or get breakfast. Hmmm. What's a girl to do?" I threw off my covers. They landed half on Dylan. Before I could get up, he snagged me around the waist. He didn't pull me anywhere, and his face was planted in the mattress next to my hip.

"Not hung over."

I chuckled. "The lack of complete sentences speak for themselves."

"Saving energy to rock your world."

He had such thick, dark hair. I missed running my fingers through it, so I did that now. "I don't have time. How about later, after Kiss Me Goodnight plays? We can go off together and talk about how we want us to be."

He shifted, rolling so that his body snaked around mine and his head rested on my lap. He peered up at me with clear eyes. Bastard hadn't been nearly as drunk as he'd let on. He'd just wanted to sleep next to me. I didn't mind that so much.

"Promise? You and me and no interruptions?"

I traced my fingertip over his stubble. "I promise."

He released me. Jane came out of the bathroom, and I took my turn. By the time I had finished, Dylan was gone.

"He said he'd see you later," Jane said. "Are you thinking you'll get back together?"

I shrugged. "I hope so. Being without him feels like a piece of me is missing." Even though he hadn't touched me, having him next to me the night before meant I'd slept deeply for the first time since I'd fallen asleep with him on my sofa.

"I'm glad you're getting back to solid footing," Luma added. "Because we're meeting Steve and Patrick after breakfast, and Thomas is with them."

I knew Luma had been in communication with Thomas, but she'd only seen him once since the Boston show. "Are you nervous?"

"A little. I mean, I listened to you talk about how amazing he was, and I kind of thought you were exaggerating, but it turns out you weren't. Then I think about the fact that you two dated—I know you didn't sleep together—and I get self-conscious."

"Don't be." I shook my head. "Even when I was dating Thomas, my heart and soul belonged to Dylan. I tried to force it because he's such a great guy, but it didn't work out. You deserve him, Luma. He'll treat you well."

The knock at the door turned out to be India. Her hair was still fire-engine red, but she'd traded her all-black stage look for mostly black mixed with some bold colors. Jane had worked with her to get her to realize that, as the lead singer, she was the face of the band. She had to stand out and be memorable. Their music was great, so now we had to make sure the rest of their package was salable.

"You guys ready?" India motioned down the hall where the rest of the band waited at the elevator.

"Yep," Jane said. "Let's get some breakfast."

The girls were nervous, which I totally understood. Once we made it to the ground floor restaurant, I ordered food for them, even though all four claimed to not be hungry.

"You'll thank her later," Jane said. "Lacey's done this before."

I figured sharing my experiences might help. "The first time Kiss Me Goodnight opened for AFI, Dylan was sick to his stomach. I had to pour Pedialyte down him so he could get on the stage. Levi spent far too much time in the bathroom—to the point where I asked if his arm was getting tired—and Daisy turned into a whip-cracking boss lady."

They laughed at the part about Levi. Bree shook her head. Like Violet and Charlotte, she'd opted to wear an A-line dress with leggings. Each had chosen a different color. Violet went with purple (the only other color besides black she liked). Charlotte had opted for a soft yellow that made her green eyes stand out. Bree had gone with electric blue. I thought the color washed her out, but I wasn't going to say that right now.

"I can see where that might be calming," Bree said. "I'm about ready to grab the next guy that walks by."

As the next guy who walked by had a huge pot belly and appeared to be north of sixty, she ended up not grabbing him.

"What about Gavin?" Jane said. "Was he calm, cool, and collected?"

The more I got to know Gavin, the more I understood how much he buried his emotions. He was the kind who suffered after-ward, when it was finished and he felt safe enough to relax. I usually tried to give him some time alone after a show so he could pull himself together.

This also wasn't a rumor I wanted to start. I spread butter on my hash browns. "He seemed unaffected, probably because he assumed the lotus position and meditated every time he felt anxious." That had meant he spent most of the day folded up and breathing with his eyes closed.

Jane considered this. "He told me to do that when I was waiting to take the bar exam. It worked."

We chatted a lot more, cracking jokes and trying to keep the girls from getting too keyed up. Then we took them to the festival and turned them over to the people who would get them where they needed to be.

Without those four anxious girls around, the tension we'd been carrying slid away. At least it did for me. Jane and Luma remained restless. This would be the first time a band they represented performed in front of a large audience.

Luma's phone vibrated. She read her text and looked around. "They're supposed to be by the concession stand."

Jane and I aided in the search. A small crowd was gathering, though most of the people milled about by the booths, shopping the various vendors. I spotted them first. Thomas had a handsome, friendly face that leapt out of any crowd.

"There they are." I pointed. They saw me and waved, which helped short little Luma home in on them.

Patrick and Steve are a cute couple, the kind who hold hands and touch frequently. And they match. Not only do they dress alike — and by that, I mean they have a similar style — but they have similar builds. Thomas did not match. He was taller, slimmer, and impeccably dressed. For this occasion, he wore a pale gray cotton shirt, and he'd left the first few buttons open. He wore shorts. I'd never seen him in shorts before, though we hadn't started dating until the fall, so I wouldn't have had the opportunity.

He looked cute, but way too uptight. If I'd met him today, I wouldn't have looked twice. Plus, he wasn't Dylan. That has always been his biggest drawback.

Luma lit up like a California wildfire. Jane and I followed her over.

"You know," Jane said. "This leaves me the odd woman out, the only one without a boyfriend. I feel kind of lonely."

I couldn't blow off Dylan tonight, not that she was asking me to. "I bet you could hang out with Levi and Gavin. Daisy, Audra, and Monty will probably be with them. They'd welcome you."

By the time we made it to where the guys were waiting, Luma and Thomas were lip-locked. I greeted Patrick and Steve with hugs. "The show should start in twenty minutes. The stage is set, and it looks like they're doing a sound check now."

In the midst of *check, check* and *one-two, one-two,* Steve laid out the details of the deal he thought he'd offer Something Wicked. They were standard terms, and I didn't see where we had leverage to negotiate for anything more. Jane asked a lot of questions, and I listened closely. Though I'd already gone this route with KMG, I was always looking to learn new things.

Some of her questions addressed crap I truly did not understand. I was glad once again I'd used her as a paid consultant before advising Kiss Me Goodnight to sign their contract.

Something Wicked came on at exactly one o'clock. I like a prompt band. It shows integrity and that they value their fans. Also, the event organizers would boot them off the stage at exactly one thirty, no matter when they'd gone on. They hadn't amassed a huge following yet—as evidenced by their position on an auxiliary stage at the edge of the festival, but they were well on their way.

India's vocals were tough when they needed to be and surprisingly tender at the right moments. I was swept away, more so than usual. It wasn't until after the performance that I noticed Dylan and crew in the front of the crowd, cheering for Something Wicked.

He'd turned out to support my band. My heart melted.

Dylan found me afterward, though Monty got to me first. He gave me a reserved hug, one that showed he'd found his inner coolness and wasn't going to taint it by hugging his aunt too effusively in public.

"They were great, Aunt Lacey. Violet is only six years older than me. Do you think she goes for younger men?"

Daisy tousled her son's hair. "She probably wants men who at least have a driver's license. Or maybe those who are allowed to date, which you are not."

I introduced everybody around, though Steve had seen Kiss Me Goodnight perform before, so he already knew who they were.

Dylan tapped my arm. "Is that Thomas over there with his face glued to Luma's?"

"Yep. They hooked up when we went to Boston."

His eyebrows lifted. "Really?"

Suddenly shy, I looked at his shoes. They were new. "You don't have to ask anymore. I've stopped lying."

"No, I meant that as a statement of disbelief. I thought you guys had some kind of code about not touching each other's exes."

I tilted my head and peered up at him. "That's *you* guys, not *us* guys. This situation hasn't come up before, but she asked if I minded, and I don't. If they make each other happy, I can't begrudge that. He's not my type anyway."

Dylan nodded. "They look good together. Complete opposites. He's this uptight suit-and-tie guy, and she's a muumuu-wearing free spirit. I think it could work."

"She comes from the same world as me. And you said he and I wouldn't work because we were from two different worlds."

He lifted a shoulder nonchalantly. "I said that because I wanted you to be with me. Still do." He brushed a strand of hair away from my face. "We're still on for tonight?"

"Yeah."

"Are you coming to see us play?"

Even when I hadn't been on speaking terms with the band, I'd planned to see them. This was their biggest accomplishment to date, and I wanted to be there, whether they knew it or not.

"Absolutely."

He wanted to kiss me. I wanted him to kiss me. He leaned down, his lips aiming for and closing in on mine. Then his chin bashed into my nose. We pitched backward, knocking into Gavin, who steadied us.

Dylan set me on my feet with one hand and turned to issue a scathing rebuke, but whoever had crashed into us was gone. He turned back to me, a wrinkle of concern on his brow. "Are you okay?"

I rubbed my nose. It was tingly, and it felt larger than normal. "I think this is karma getting me back for the time I punched you."

He tilted my head back and checked out my face. "Nah. No blood. Looks like karma's waiting a little longer."

India and the rest of the ladies from Something Wicked tried to push through the crowd to us but found themselves surrounded by new fans. I watched as they signed flyers and shirts, and at least one man asked to have his chest signed.

I set my hand on Dylan's shoulder and leaned against his side, stealing a public cuddle. "I'm so glad you never signed anybody's chest."

He fidgeted. "I wouldn't say that."

I wanted to put my hands on my hips and get all huffy on him, but I had no right. Not only had we broken up, but I'd let Thomas put his arms around me and pretend I was with him so he could save face in front of his ex-girlfriend.

Settling for the next best thing, I squeezed his bicep. "We can say you'll never do it again."

He kissed the tip of my nose, which felt fine now. "We can say that. Unless it's your chest. I'd sign there."

This whole time, Jane and Steve had been hammering out the details of the contract. Luma and I had abdicated our responsibilities in favor of spending time with our love interests. The fact that Jane didn't say anything or throw it in our faces spoke volumes about her character. She was a true friend. When she met somebody wonderful, I vowed to make sure she had ample time and opportunity to pursue him. Or her. I still wasn't sold on Jane being exclusively heterosexual.

Daisy, Levi, and Gavin closed in, surrounding me with the first band I'd ever loved as family. They stared at me until I became self-conscious, which happened quickly. When four people you've lied about — even if you've apologized and been forgiven — surround you, it's not too dramatic to experience unease.

"We want you back," Gavin said.

"Yeah," Levi agreed. "We miss you." He elbowed Daisy.

"As our manager," she added, rubbing her rib. "You were great at representing us. We suck at something you made look so easy."

I hadn't found it difficult. Challenging and time-intensive, yes, but not a hardship. I'd loved touting their music to the world. Would I come back? Hell, yes. "It wouldn't be just me," I said. "It would be LJL Talent. Jane will draw up a contract and get that to you within a week. Then we'll sit down and see where you are and where you need to be."

"Sounds great," Levi said. "So, that means Luma will handle the public relations part? You won't be talking to the press anymore?"

Heat stained my chest and traveled up my neck to my face. I wanted to blame the August sun, but there was no getting around my chagrin. "Yes. I'm strictly a behind-the-scenes person now, which is what I prefer."

By the time Something Wicked made it to us, the next band was taking the stage. The four girls — *women*; I needed to stop calling them girls — hugged their way through Kiss Me Goodnight.

Daisy plucked at her boys. (Yes, I have no problem calling Dylan, Levi, and Gavin *boys*.) Anyway, she herded them away from us. "We'll see you later," she said. "Monty, let's go."

Monty protested. He wanted to see the current band. He looked to me to save him.

"Sorry. I have work to do."

Audra slung her arm around Monty. "You know, I'm feeling a little unloved here. You could ask me to hang out with you. It's not like I'm managing a band or sneaking in one last rehearsal."

Monty put his arm around Audra, tucking the tiny blonde to his side. "Okay, but if anybody asks, you're my sister. It's not cool to hang out with your mother."

Audra beamed. It occurred to me that Audra had come into Monty's life when he was six years old. That age had been a time of change for him too—good change. He'd gained a parent who loved him with all her heart. It also occurred to me that he didn't have a problem referring to her as his mother. My chest constricted as I realized how I'd deprived John of that joy.

If I had it all to do again, I wouldn't make the same selfish mistakes. But we all say that, don't we? Hindsight and all that. At least I take comfort in knowing that John understood. Words from the letter he'd written me flashed through my memory:

Know that I will never leave your side. I might not be there in body, but I'll always be there in spirit. I love you, Lacey. You might not have called me "Dad," but you are my little girl. You always will be.

He was here with me, sharing in my accomplishments, my trials and triumphs. I knew he was proud that I'd changed my name. Better late than never.

Kiss Me Goodnight went off to practice, and Audra took Monty closer to the stage. India hugged me so tight, I thought I might need medical attention to remove my ribs from my internal organs.

"Thank you, Lacey. I know you're the one who arranges all the tour dates. I doubted you at first, and I'm sorry."

"You doubted me?" I injected as much dramatic irony into that as I could. I'd also doubted them. I pressed my hand to my heart and pretended to swoon. Then I righted myself, instantly over it. "Come over here. I want to introduce you to somebody."

I gathered the band around me. "Steve, I'd like you to meet India, Bree, Charlotte, and Violet of Something Wicked. Ladies, I'd like you to meet Steve Aubrey. He's with Virgin."

They shook hands and exchanged pleasantries. Charlotte and Bree were actually shaking. They clasped each other's hands tightly.

"We'd like to offer you a contract," Steve said. "Jane and I are still working on the details, but we should have something soon."

Shrieking. Jumping up and down. I moved away to save my eardrums. Glancing around, I realized we'd lost somebody. Luma and Thomas had disappeared. I figured Jane and I should avoid our hotel room for a few hours.

"Well, it looks like you have nothing but free time on your hands for the rest of the festival. Enjoy, ladies. Celebrate the fact that you completely rocked today."

Jane and I hung out with Steve and Patrick for the afternoon. Luma and Thomas joined us about the time we headed over to the second stage to see Kiss Me Goodnight. We teased them mercilessly, and they took it with numerous blushes, cocky grins, and shared looks. I couldn't remember the last time I'd seen Luma so lovestruck. Thomas either, for that matter.

A large crowd had amassed to see Kiss Me Goodnight. If my calculations were correct, this was twice the size of their last concert, though it was still small compared to what they would've had at the main stage. Oh, well. It was a goal to strive toward for next year. No, I wanted the organizers to beg us next year. Yeah, that's the goal I set. Lofty, I know, but if I'm not going to make up things about the past anymore, I figure I can do it for the future.

The concert was excellent. They played through their new record, and Dylan did a nice job of stopping between numbers to talk to the crowd. I knew he was getting them worked up for the last number. They'd stopped ending with the song from which they took their name. Now that honor went to "Wrong Name."

It's funny. That song had caused me so much pain and heartache, but thinking about it right now didn't fill me with the intense anxiety it used to.

Near the end of their allotted stage time, Dylan came to the front. He slapped hands with people in the first few rows. Then he stood and got serious. "Ladies and gentlemen, I want to thank you for coming out. We wouldn't be here if it weren't for you, but there's one person who brought us to you. She believed in us from the very beginning. She's been our biggest cheerleader, and she's become family to us all. Lacey Zimmerman, this next song—it's brand-spanking new—goes out to you."

It's in the way she smiles
The curl of her hair that won't stay behind her ear
The hitch in her breath when I'm near
It's in the way she kisses
That look in her eyes — It makes me real
The strength of her sighs — It makes me real

I'm not losing you, baby
You're everything to me
I'm not losing, losing you.

It's in the way she screams my name
Cherry lip gloss on my tongue
Making me crazy for some…love
Oh, baby, when you turned away, my world stopped cold
Every day without your smile, pieces of me disappeared
I'll do anything to get you back
Because, Lacey, I'm not losing you.

Parts of the song were slow and soulful, while others were screamed with heartfelt emotion. Gavin and Daisy sang backing vocals, repeating "It makes me real" at strategic points throughout the song. It sent shivers up my spine. Daisy had a damn good singing voice. I hoped one day to get her to take lead or do a few duets.

I don't know how many people caught the fact that he substituted "Lacey" for "baby" before the last repetition of the chorus, and I didn't care. This song was Dylan's declaration of love for me. By the time he finished, tears ran down my cheeks.

Jane gave me a hug. "I guess he's not losing you. How do you feel about that?"

Pretty damn good, but I was so choked up that I could only nod.

The crowd cheered, but the noise died down when Dylan introduced the next song. "This last song does *not* go out to Lacey. It's for anybody who's ever fucked up royally."

I liked that introduction for "Wrong Name." He had fucked up royally, and the ripple effects from it had taken almost a year to dissipate.

Once they finished, I texted Dylan that I would meet him at the hotel. Many fans were waiting around to see KMG, and I knew he'd be a little while. Then he'd want to shower, which was fine by me because he could rock some wicked body odor after a performance in the hot August sun.

I wanted to freshen up and take care of some loose ends. Luma and Thomas had slipped away during the performance, and I figured I knew where they'd gone, so I didn't bother them. Jane and I returned to the hotel together and hoped Luma and Thomas were decently clothed by the time we got there. I texted Luma to let her know we were on our way, but I didn't hear back.

The elevator opened on our floor. Jane stepped out first. "Should we knock or just go in?"

If Luma was with anybody else, I would have voted to go in without knocking. "Knock. That's not a conversation I want to have with Dylan tonight."

Though he'd seemed totally relaxed about Thomas being with Luma earlier, I wanted no opportunity for a misunderstanding with Dylan. I was tired of fighting. I missed the hell out of him, and I wanted to get to the kiss-and-make-up phase. Not trusting Jane (because under any other circumstances, we'd both find it funny to catch them au natural), I did the honors.

No answer. I pressed my ear to the door, but I couldn't hear the sounds of scrambling. "Looks like it's option two."

We went inside and found the room empty. Jane shrugged. "They're not here. Go ahead and pretty yourself up for your man. I'll pick your outfit."

Jane's sense of style and mine were at opposite ends of the spectrum. She favored bright colors, and she didn't have a problem mixing stripes and prints. I often had a problem wearing stripes *or* prints. Her offer caused me no small amount of panic.

"Okay, but you're limited to what's in my suitcase." I hadn't brought date clothes, but I felt reasonably comfortable my outfit would end up matching.

I washed my hair. I figured I had the time, so I might as well. My curls had a window of greatness that began an hour after I washed them and expired about four hours later. In the summer humidity, I might get only three hours out of my hair before all products wore off and it hit maximum frizz levels. I would bring a hair tie just in case. Dylan likes when I have a big, bushy ponytail. He says it's like hogtied sex hair, and it shows off my sexy neck, and it gives him ideas and urges. I generally like his ideas and urges, so I often wear a ponytail when we're going out. Yep, I'm a tease. He likes that about me too.

Jane chose a pair of denim shorts that emphasized my luscious backside and the shape of my legs. They're my favorite. She paired them with a shirt that hugged my torso and had billowy sleeves with cut-out shoulders. It wasn't mine. Jane had purloined it from Luma's bag. We both knew she wouldn't mind.

Jane winked as she gave it to me. "It'll give Dylan something to do with his mouth when he's done begging you to get back with him."

"He's begged enough. That song was amazing." I whipped off my baby tee and slid into Luma's sultry little number. She must have known Thomas might be here, because it wasn't the only sexy piece she'd brought along.

"You guys have some hard topics to discuss," she said. "You both owe apologies."

I nodded, but I hoped our wrongs had canceled each other out.

Jane disappeared into the bathroom, so I wandered down the hall to see if More Than Swagger were in their room. They badly needed to practice before their performance tomorrow morning. They had the worst time slot all weekend. Most people who came to Lollapalooza didn't get a three-day pass, and those who did weren't usually up and about at ten in the morning the day after the festival's Saturday-night headliner performed. I would only be there because I represented More Than Swagger. Dylan, I knew, would be there to support me. I think he liked Ari and Leo well enough. He didn't really know Max or Bastien, but he'd probably like them if that fact changed.

I heard voices coming from their room. Leo answered. "Hey, Lacey." He threw open the door. He'd beaten tracks in his dark hair. Pieces of it stuck up, but he made it look charming.

"Hi, Leo. I stopped by to see how things were going."

He shrugged. "Crappy. Bennett's still MIA, and Violet just got here. We're thinking we should pull out of this, but at the same time, we're afraid it would be career suicide."

Having Bennett in their band was career suicide. I gave him a sympathetic squeeze on the shoulder. "You need a new drummer."

"We know." Ari sat on the edge of the bed, utter desolation turning his brown eyes black. "Right now, we're just focusing on getting through tomorrow. There's no way Violet can learn all eight songs, so we're trying to simplify the beat."

"It makes the songs suck," Max said.

I didn't know anybody with a drum machine they could borrow. Violet had her practice pad and her sticks. She whacked a good beat on them. "We'll be okay. It won't be great, but next time people see you, they'll hear the improvement."

Bastien sat in front of his keyboard, staring at the settings. It wasn't fancy enough to do double duty. "If Bennett comes back here, I might beat the shit out of him."

I wanted to offer assurances, but I had none. "Don't beat him up. Kick him out. Tell him he's done, but don't beat him up. He's not worth the assault charge."

Violet studied me intently. "You look cute. Hot date?"

"Yeah. Dylan."

She grinned. "If he sang that song to me, I'd forgive him for being a dick too."

"He wasn't—" I wanted to defend him, but I realized Violet only knew he'd left me stranded, not about everything else. I aimed to keep it that way. "We both did things we regret. Please don't think the worst of him."

She shrugged. "It was nice of him to show up and support us. They put us on their Facebook page and Twitter feed. We got a lot of nice compliments and people asking where they can download singles."

"Luma should have issued that information already. If not, she'll get to it before long." I made a mental note to send her a text. She'd eventually need to take a break. Even a stallion needs time to recover. I edged toward the exit. "I'll leave you guys to work it out. If you need something, call Jane."

Nobody answered at Dylan's room, but I heard the shower, so I assumed he was still getting ready. My room was down the hall next to the stairwell. I hated that, because we heard people coming and going at all hours of the night, especially the drunk or giggly ones making an ice run. Plus we could hear the clink of ice and the grinding of the machine's motor in our room.

The heavy door at the end of the hall opened as I approached my room, and I did a double take. Bennett stood in the doorway, alone, and he'd cleaned up. His sandy brown hair had been recently combed, and his clothes were fresh.

"Bennett! Where have you been? Everybody's worried." I didn't say they were worried for his health and welfare, because that would be a lie.

"Can I talk to you?" He was calm, and his tone seemed contrite. He folded his hands in front of him and kept his gaze on the floor.

This was the likeable Bennett I'd glimpsed on occasion, though I didn't exactly trust him to stay that way. "Sure. What's up?"

He motioned to the stairwell. "It's not exactly private, but there's less traffic."

Until later, when everybody moved the parties to their rooms… He held the door open, and I went through. The vending and ice machines were recessed in an alcove off the landing. It gave us a little out-of-the-way area for our conversation. I took a deep breath to calm my nerves and make sure the rational part of my brain was in control.

"Bennett, tell me what's going on with you." *And make it short. The last time I planned to spend the evening with Dylan, you fucked it up for me.*

He swayed, shattering any illusion that he was sober. "You told them to kick me out of the band."

I'd presented it as an alternative to Bastien being arrested for battery. But the door had been open, so if Bennett had been in the hall, he could've overheard. Still, if they were smart, they'd follow my advice. I hadn't the patience or inclination to coddle Bennett. "They're going to suck tomorrow, and it's your fault. You don't take this seriously. You treat practice as a joke. You're more concerned with partying and getting laid than with perfecting your craft."

Lips twisted bitterly, he stepped closer. His eyes blazed, and he loomed over me. "You gave Something Wicked a better time slot and stage than us. We never had a chance because you treated us like we were nothing from the beginning. We changed our fucking *name* for you, and you screwed us like pussies."

I recognized now that Bennett had not only been drinking, but he was on something else as well. Figuring out which drug he'd taken seemed less important than getting back into the hallway where people were more likely to be present. My heart beat faster as I recognized the danger I was in. I tried sidling toward the door, but Bennett smashed me against the ice machine. My head knocked against it, and the lever pressed into my lower back. Now I *really* hated that thing, and I'd firmly decided I did not like Bennett.

"You were against me from the beginning. I coulda been good to you. One night with me, and you would've begged for more, but I wasn't famous enough, was I? Where's your rock star boyfriend now? Probably getting a blowjob from a groupie while you're stuck back here waiting for leftovers. I woulda never done that, not with a piece of ass as sweet as you."

"Bennett, back up. This conversation is over." I may not have had the upper hand, but that wouldn't stop me from pretending I did.

He responded by flattening me between his body and the cold machine. In my whole life, I'd never been in a situation like this. I'd never even lied about being in a situation like this. Fear knifed through my veins, icy and hot, making me temporarily numb.

"Say *pretty please*."

I was *not* going to beg. I was going to introduce his balls to his throat as soon as I had an opening. My senses might have been a tad addled from the knock on my head, but they were also curiously sharper. Strategies percolated through my mind, but most involved lying — or worse, begging, and that was something I suddenly couldn't do.

"Fuck off, Bennett." Somewhere I'd read that I should keep using his name. Or was that in hostage negotiations? Keep using the victim's name so the captor sees them as a person? I couldn't remember, but I figured it couldn't hurt my cause, and maybe it would help keep me from freaking out.

He cupped my breast and kneaded it in his hand. Then he leaned down, putting his face closer to mine. "I'm gonna show you what you're missing."

Ignoring the fact that the bastard was pawing my woman parts, I head-butted him in the nose. Blood spurted, spraying at me, and you know how I react to that, right? My fight-or-flight response withered in the face of a little blood. Or a lot. He slapped his hand over the geyser, and I tried desperately to control my breathing. Now was not the time to pass out. Sounds became distant. Somewhere below us, I heard a door slam.

Bennett swore, calling me all sorts of names that meant nothing coming from him. I have a vague recollection of him grabbing me by the arms and shaking me. My head might or might not have bounced against the ice machine.

When I came to, the floor was hard underneath me, like concrete covered with carpet. I deduced I was lying in the stairwell. My head hurt, and I didn't want to open my eyes. The lids were too heavy anyway. I let my other senses return first. Somebody was messing with my clothes.

"Lacey? Damn it. Please wake up. Jane, tell the paramedics to hurry. There's blood all over her face and down her shirt, but I can't find the source." Dylan's voice came at me through a tunnel.

"Okay," I mumbled. Other than the sound of his voice, I wasn't sure what I was responding to.

"I'm here, Lace. You're safe. The medics are on their way upstairs."

"Bennett." I wanted to let him know who had done this to me. I wasn't sure what was wrong. The back of my skull throbbed. "He was mad. Drunk. On drugs."

"Bennett did this to you?" Layers of suppressed fury turned his tone deadly. "What did he do, Lacey? Tell me how he hurt you."

I managed to pry my eyes open. Dampness made Dylan's hair darker than normal, and his eyes were cloudy with worry. "Ruined my night. I wanted to spend it with you."

He laughed, but I think it was with relief. "We can reschedule. First we're taking you to the hospital, and we'll notify the police that you were attacked by that motherfucker. There's time to figure out the rest later, okay?"

My eyelids were impossibly weighty. I tried to nod, but I don't know how successful I was. I stopped fighting, and my eyelids slipped down.

"No, Lacey, don't go to sleep." Dylan shook my shoulder.

"Lacey!" Jane yelled in my face.

"I'm not deaf," I whispered. "My head hurts, and my eyes don't want to stay open."

"Where does your head hurt?" Jane asked.

"Back. Front. He shoved me against the ice machine, but it didn't hurt so much at the time. I head-butted him in the nose, and then I passed out when I saw the blood."

"This is his blood?" Dylan asked gently.

I smiled at the effort he put into keeping calm for me. "Yep. Shit. Jane, Luma's going to be mad about her shirt."

Jane chuckled, but there was no mirth in it. "She'll be relieved that you're okay."

"Dylan?"

He squeezed my hand. "I'm here."

I forced my eyes to open, but I couldn't make them focus. The effort made me forget what I had wanted to say. After searching my head and coming up with nada, I said the only thing I could think of. "I think I have a concussion. This does not mean you get to move in with me."

He and Jane both laughed, and this time, I heard real relief.

"I know to ask first," he said. "The paramedics are here now. They're going to get you stabilized."

"Stay with me," I said as a woman and a man in uniform knelt over me. They shot questions to Dylan and Jane. Dylan didn't answer me, but he never left my side.

Chapter Twelve

Twelve hours later, medical personnel confirmed that I had a mild concussion, most likely from head-butting Bennett. Though I did have tenderness at the back of my head where I'd hit the ice machine, most of my trauma was high on my forehead. Thank goodness for bangs.

I filed a police report, and Bennett was found later in the same ER. He had a broken nose, two black eyes, and he was down one tooth. I'd hit him hard, so I guess my fight-or-flight response had chosen to kick ass and pass out.

The good news? I got so used to seeing blood as they cleaned it off me and I tried to wash it out of Luma's shirt that it no longer took my consciousness. It still affected me, but now I could look at it with a certain amount of detachment.

Dylan remained at my side, which was good because I think he might've killed Bennett if he'd found him before the police, especially after he heard the statement I gave. He talked to me in a soothing tone, keeping the subject matter light and friendly. We did not discuss weighty topics, though I knew they pressed on both our minds.

I made Jane and Luma go see More Than Swagger perform while I took a much-needed nap in our hotel room. Dylan stayed with me, and I slept in his arms. It was like coming home.

We had to be out of the room by two, so Jane and Luma returned at one. I appreciated the extra hours of rest. When I got up to pack my things, Dylan tried to make me sit down.

"I'm fine," I said. "Just a little tired. Jane's driving home, so I'll sleep in the car."

"I'll pack your stuff." He took my shampoo bottle from me.

"Go pack your own stuff. You have to be out at the same time." I felt frustrated, and it was getting out of control. Rationally, I knew this was a small issue, but my brain wouldn't move past the fact that he was coddling me, and I didn't like it.

"More Than Swagger did not rock the stage," Luma said. She was trying to distract Dylan and me from our disagreement. "We cut them loose. I told Ari and Leo that if they formed a more stable lineup, they should give us a call."

Jane snorted. "I think they understood that Bennett would not be welcomed back, even if he begged on his hands and knees."

While I agreed, I felt irritable and contrary, so I kept my mouth shut.

Luma sighed and sat on the edge of the bed next to me. "I think the moral of this story is that if all three of us aren't one-hundred-percent on board with a band, we don't sign them. You were right, Lacey. They didn't have what it takes, and Something Wicked developed just like you said they would."

Dylan zipped my suitcase and grinned. "She has great instincts. Just keep her away from bloggers."

"I don't do badly with bloggers." I scowled. Lying was in my past, but I was going to have to prove myself to my friends and loved ones once again. Having been through this before, I didn't relish the process. Being doubted sucked, and though I had it coming, it still pissed me off.

"It's the concussion," Dylan said, interrupting my internal tirade. "Expect irrational mood swings. Give it a week or so to heal. It should get better each day."

The knock on the door turned out to be Daisy. "I've packed your things, little brother. It's time to hit the road." She peered at me, looking way too motherly. At least she didn't feel my forehead for a fever. "How are you feeling?"

"Like I nailed a jerk in the face with my head."

She laughed. "Dylan, are you going back with them or us?"

Dylan looked at me, and I could tell he wanted to ride with us. I shook my head. "I'm going to stretch out in the back seat and sleep. You'll just get in the way."

"Actually," Luma said, "I'm not going back with you. Thomas is taking me to Boston so we can spend some time together. There's plenty of room for Dylan."

Well, that was a neat solution. I shrugged. "I'm still sleeping."

Daisy put a suitcase down inside our room. "Here's your stuff. I'll see you when I see you. Don't forget to call and let me know how Lacey's doing and if you need anything." Then she gave me a tight hug. "You scared the shit out of us. Monty wants to see you before we go. Are you okay with that?"

I peered at her, and then I glanced at Dylan. "Do I look that bad?"

"You look a little rough," he said, "but not bad."

"Monty can come in." It would be cruel to deny him.

He must have been listening in the hall, because he flew inside. The next thing I knew, he was kneeling on the floor with his arms around my waist and his head in my lap. I stroked his hair and hoped I was soothing him.

"I'm okay," I assured him.

He stayed like that for several long moments. Then he lifted his head and got to his feet. "We're still on for lunch Wednesday, right?"

"You bet." I hadn't been aware we had a date, but I wasn't going to deny him anything right now. He might have known that.

He kissed my cheek. Thomas came to pick up Luma, and then I was alone with Jane and Dylan.

"Let's get going," Jane said. She picked up her suitcase. Dylan took his and mine. Over her shoulder, she shot him a challenge with the lift of her brow. "Are you up for taking a driving shift, or are you too worn out?"

They'd both stayed with me in the ER, so I knew Jane was as wiped out as Dylan. Still, he'd never met a challenge he couldn't make his bitch. "I'll take first shift. I napped this morning with Lacey. You can get some sleep."

I don't remember the trip home, only Dylan rousing me when we got to my place. He stayed with me that night to make sure I was all right, but he went home the next morning without me having to kick him out.

A few days later, we all gathered at Daisy's house. Jane had the contract Kiss Me Goodnight could sign to have LJL Talent represent them. My head was feeling much better, and I hadn't been irrationally angry since that first day.

I had a dark bruise on my forehead, so I definitely wore my bangs down. That didn't stop everybody from moving them aside and commenting on my battle wound, calling me terms of endearment like *hammerhead* and *crusher*.

Once the signing was completed—which took all of two minutes, even though the terms included a larger percentage for LJL than it had for just me—the place erupted in hugs. After a celebratory round of sparkling cider (it was the middle of the day, people), Jane and I left. We took Monty out for a late lunch and let the band rehearse. I'd already booked the first leg of their tour. They were going to need a larger rehearsal space. It might be prudent for LJL to start socking funds away to purchase a place for bands to practice and record demos.

Dylan picked me up at six for our rescheduled date. He took me out to dinner at a fancy restaurant, and then we hit the freeway for a long drive. I recognized the park as soon as we arrived. He'd taken me here last summer to show me the stars.

"The last time I came here was with you," he said. "Can you grab the flashlight out of the glove box?"

Though the sun had not yet set, it was well on its way down. I eagerly grabbed the flashlight, as I did not want to be stranded out here at night without a light source. In the distance, a coyote howled. It was a sound I'd heard only in movies.

"We have coyotes in Michigan?"

He slung a backpack over his shoulder and locked up his truck. "Yep. Don't worry; they'll avoid us. Or you'll head-butt them. Either way, I'll be safe."

"You're the guy," I said as he chuckled at his joke. "You're supposed to protect me from wild animals."

He held my hand and led me to the trail head. "You're pretty badass. I feel confident you can keep us safe."

"Dylan…"

"Relax. I'll keep you safe. Oh—there's a place where the trail gets narrow and the edge drops off. Be careful."

Now he warns me. Last time, I nearly met my demise at that blind corner. "Thanks. Good to know." With his sense of humor, he was lucky he wrote such sweet songs about me.

We strolled down the trail, watching the last traces of light disappear from the canopy. The woods at twilight were eerily beautiful. "Daisy used to bring you here at night?"

"She did."

"You weren't scared?"

"Nope. I knew she wouldn't let anything happen to me, just like you know I won't let anything happen to you." He drew me closer as we came to the place where the side of the trail dropped away.

I peered over it and realized it wasn't as deep as I'd originally thought. Still, it would be a nasty fall. We took the path to the bottom, and he spread a blanket on the shore of the stream. He sat down, cross-legged, and patted the place next to him. I sat.

"Do you remember what I said the first time I brought you here?"

He'd told me about losing his parents. We held hands and looked at the stars. "You said you liked me."

He took my hand, kissed the palm, and set it on his thigh. "I still do. Do you still like me?"

"Yes." I played along. "I really like you."

"After all we've put each other through, you still like me?" Stars popped out above us, but his gaze demanded my attention.

"Yeah. I even still love you."

"I love you too." He stared at me, searching my face for something. "What happened to us? Where did we go wrong?"

I shook my head. It had been a confluence of events, not anything specific. "My mom said we both approached our relationship from an immature standpoint. She said you need to learn that a relationship is about two people, what they both need and want, not just you." He winced at that, but I barreled forward. Mom hadn't restricted her criticism to Dylan's behavior. "She said I use hand washing and lying as a crutch and a defense mechanism. I push people away and sabotage relationships that get too emotionally risky. She said that's why I chose to date married men. They were emotionally unavailable, so not risky."

His chuckle was full of irony. "Daisy said the same thing, just not so nicely."

"I know. She told me to put on my big-girl panties. By the way, I'm not wearing any tonight." And I was wearing a dress. I knew he'd like that. The nice dinner hadn't been a surprise, but our return to the trail had been.

He groaned and rubbed his hand over mine. When he spoke, his voice was a little hoarse, and I knew he was struggling to keep his mind on our conversation. I resisted the urge to goad him by cupping my hand over where I knew he had a bulge.

"She told me off too, after I broke it off the second time because you had to babysit a band. I got used to having you devote your time and attention to me. You were *my* girlfriend, and you represented *my* band. Then suddenly I wasn't the center of your world anymore, and I got jealous. Insanely, foolishly jealous."

"The things I said didn't help."

"No, they certainly didn't. But you've really turned that around. Your hands aren't red or chapped, and you haven't lied in months. Those are huge accomplishments, Lacey. I'm proud of you. I always knew you were strong enough to beat this."

"And pushing you away when you were feeling insecure really messed things up."

He put his arm around me and scooted me closer to him. "I didn't tell you what I was feeling, and it wasn't fair for me to expect you to structure your life around me. I can be a bit self-centered at times."

At times. I loved his qualification. "Yeah, but I don't mind it so much. It's part of what I love about you, the way you decide you want something and go for it. Moving in with me, expecting me to be at your beck and call…It wasn't different; it was just too much. I feel a little hypocritical asking you to change."

Now his arms were completely around me. I was mostly in his lap. He traced his thumb over my lower lip. "Why? You changed for me. I mean, you did it for yourself, but you did it so we could be together. I can change for you—grow as a person. I know I move too fast. I'm not without baggage. Losing my parents so young makes me anxious to rebuild my family, and I want to do that with you. Only it doesn't occur to me to ask you if you want the same things. I make assumptions, and that's wrong. I can talk to you, ask you for what I want, tell you when I need more from you. We can communicate like mature people."

I wiggled the rest of the way onto his lap. Sliding my hands up his chest, I worked my way to the buttons on his dress shirt. "I think I'm going to like being mature with you."

Spreading his hands wide, he moved them up my back. I liked the way it made me feel possessed and treasured. "How mature did you want to get?"

He'd removed his tie in the truck. I worked on his buttons. Since the sun had dipped below the horizon, I had to feel my way. "Very mature. Adult movie mature. X-rated. Pornographic."

Gripping my hips, he ground me against him. "Not pornographic. Those women are too bossy. 'From the front,'" he mimicked in a high-pitched voice. "'Now turn around. Faster. Harder. Stop. Reposition. Start again.' They never give a man time to get going."

I laughed. Dylan was the only man I knew who openly disliked porn movies. I'd looked at his eReader often enough to know he read romances, especially erotic lesbian ones, but I'd never caught him enjoying porn. I wasn't complaining, and I also enjoyed the lesbian stories.

"You take direction very well," I said. "Let's take off your shirt. I want to touch you. It's been too long, Dylan. I miss making love with you."

He let me remove his shirt, and then he lifted my dress over my head. I was wearing a bra and thigh-highs, which he explored with his hands. He fumbled for something, and then a beam of light pooled over me.

"Hot damn, Lacey. How about we do it fast and dirty out here, and then I'll take you home and make love to you with the lights on."

I ran my hands over his torso as I considered his proposal. "I don't know. It depends on how fast and how dirty."

He locked his lips to mine and flipped us so I was beneath him. He touched me everywhere, caressing with his hands and feeling his way with his lips. I was an ember, and he stoked me to a flame with his deft touch. I grasped at him, scratching passionate paths on his back and shoulders.

Since he was still wearing pants, I cupped his erection with one hand and loosened his belt with the other. Then something sharp jabbed my ass. I cried out, the wrong kind to be mistaken for passion.

He paused. "What's wrong?"

"Stick or stone. Something under this blanket isn't working with us."

"That's okay," he said. "I want you on your hands and knees anyway." He knelt and let me get into position.

"You should have said so earlier. I was ready to dry hump your leg."

"Bossy," he said, slapping my ass lightly. "This is why we're doing it fast and dirty. You're too delicate to forego a mattress."

I tried to think of a retort, but he chose that moment to slide his cock against me. It felt so good, comfortable and familiar, yet new and exciting. Anything I might have said turned into a moan. "Oh, yes. God, I missed you."

He breached my entrance, filling me with his thick length. Air hissed from between his teeth. "Damn, Lace. You're so tight. I hope you're close, because just being inside you is so fucking hot."

I braced myself. "Fast and dirty. Don't stop until I scream your name."

He was past joking about my bossiness. He gripped my shoulder with one hand and reached around to stimulate my clit with the other. I arched my back and let him take me. The roiling heat inside exploded, carrying me away on waves of bliss. Dylan came with me, or very soon after.

We collapsed on the blanket. He managed to fall so that most of his weight was on the ground. He closed his arms around me and held me so tightly that I thought I might become part of him.

"I love you, Lacey. Damn, I needed that—to be close to you, inside you, reconnecting with you."

I had needed it too. Vast emotion welled in my chest, cutting off my airflow for a second. I'd never felt this strongly about anyone. Loving Dylan used to scare me, but now it brought me comfort. Being in his arms was being home—safe, secure, and where I belong.

"I love you too, Dylan. I want you to move in with me."

He tilted my head back so that he could look into my face. The moon had come out, and I could see him clearly. A fierce light glowed in his eyes. "For real this time?"

"Your name is already on the lease." I drew my fingertip along his lip. "I'll let you rearrange the kitchen. And I left your closet space alone. There's plenty of room for your vast hoard of shoes."

He captured my finger with his teeth, scraping them along my skin and sucking on the tip. "You know all the right things to say. That's an offer I can't refuse."

I lifted my brows. "Really? Because if that didn't work, I was going to offer unlimited sexual access. I should have known appealing to your shoe fetish would seal the deal."

He got up and lifted me to my feet. "Get dressed. We're going home so I can take advantage of this unlimited sexual access thing."

I shimmied into my dress. "I didn't offer it. I said I was going to. You bit when I mentioned shoes."

He'd never completely taken off his pants, and he didn't button his shirt, so it didn't take him long to dress. I stepped off the blanket so we could fold it up, but he fumbled with the backpack instead. He took something out and set it on the blanket. "Shine the flashlight here, okay? I can't find what I need."

I wanted to get going so we could spend all night naked and sweaty. Did he *have* to fold the blanket? "Can't it wait?"

"Nope."

Reluctantly, I obliged. It turned out he'd brought his MP3 player and a portable speaker. He queued a song, and then he took the flashlight from me. In the glow of moonlight, I watched him sort through the bag. He came up with a rose, which he handed to me. "Sorry. It's a little crushed."

I studied the thing, and then I looked into the night sky where the full moon shone brightly. I'd said I wanted moonlight and roses. My heart burst at his thoughtfulness. I was ready to hug him again, but he'd started the music. Acoustic guitar drifted over to me. It was a song I hadn't heard, but I recognized Dylan's style. He got to his feet and took my hand in his.

> *The moon glints off your skin, a midnight caress from the heavens*
> *My eyes trace your curves, a promise you'd better be believing*
> *I touch your face and move a little bit closer*
> *Your eyes close, your lips part, and you wait*
> *Anticipation feels so good*
>
> *Fresh breezes hurry across the water,*
> *Lifting your hair and exposing your neck*
> *I press my lips there, inhale your pure, hot, feminine scent*
> *Your eyes close, your breath stops, and you wait*
> *Anticipation feels so good*
>
> *I kiss you by moonlight, I love you for hours*
> *Surrounded by grass and water and the scent of spring flowers*
> *I touch your face, bite your lip*
> *You writhe and moan, my hair's in your grip*
> *Scratches on my back, trails of fire from your fingertips*
> *So I kiss you by moonlight, love you for hours*

Speechless, I listened to him sing to me, baring his heart and soul as only he could. By the time he finished, my eyes were wet. I leaned in to give him a kiss.

He cradled the back of my head in his hand and traced my lips. His face tilted down, and his lips met mine in a soft caress that turned into a tongue wrangling. When he broke away, his chest was heaving. "Ten minutes, Lacey. We might have to pull off the road."

I laughed, a husky chuckle that belied my happiness and excitement. "Mmmm. More sex in a public place. You're walking on the wild side."

We traversed the trail back to the car and headed home. He held out as long as he could. I helped weaken his resolve by caressing his man parts until he squirmed in his seat. We made it about six miles down the road from our apartment when he turned onto a service road. No cars came from either direction, and the only light came from the moon and the stars…and the powerful street lights lining the road.

He unzipped his fly. "Let's test drive this unlimited sexual access thing. Hop on, Lace. Ride me like the stallion I am."

I giggled at his description. In my head, I pictured Luma challenging me to figure out which stallion had the most stamina: mine or hers. I put money on mine, mostly because I didn't care about hers.

He slid his seat back as far as it would go, and I straddled him. "It's a good thing I opted to not wear panties."

He guided himself into me, and then he held onto my hips. Dylan liked when I was on top. He'd let me play for as long as he could stand it, then he'd take control and make me scream like a banshee at a solstice celebration.

Tonight, I wasn't in the mood to play. I wanted him too much. We'd had months apart. The poor man didn't know what he was in for. I intended to ride him until his penis broke.

I set a fast pace. He made those sexy groaning noises and said my name. I pushed his shirt off his shoulders and clawed his skin. The fire between my thighs turned into an inferno that detonated in my core. I lost myself for a few moments. When I came down, Dylan had me in his arms, my head on his shoulder. He stroked a hand down my spine.

"It's okay. I've got you. I'll never let you go."

I clutched him tighter. "Promise?"

"Cross my heart. I'm not losing you, Lacey. You're mine forever."

That sounded perfect to me. I found his lips, and I kissed him in the moonlight.

Acknowledgments

I'd like to thank my awesome team of beta readers—Amy Malek Concepcion, Jennifer Diaz, and Julie B. Deaton—and everybody at Omnific who worked to bring the Kiss Me series to life.

About the Author

I'm Michele Zurlo, author of more than twenty romance novels. I write contemporary and paranormal, BDSM and mainstream — whatever it takes to give my characters the happy endings they deserve.

I'm not half as interesting as my characters. My childhood dreams tended to stretch no further than the next book in my to-be-read pile, and I aspired to be a librarian so I could read all day. I ended up teaching middle school, so that fulfilled part of my dream. Some words of wisdom from an inspiring lady had me tapping out stories on my first laptop, so these days, in the evenings, romantic tales flow from my fingertips.

I'm pretty impulsive when it comes to big decisions, especially when it's something I've never done before. Writing is just one in a long line of impulsive decisions that turned out to showcase my great instincts.☺ Find out more at www.michelezurloauthor.com or @MZurloAuthor.

check out these titles from

OMNIFIC PUBLISHING

Contemporary Romance

Boycotts & Barflies and *Trust in Advertising* by Victoria Michaels
Passion Fish by Alison Oburia and Jessica McQuinn
The Small Town Girl series: *Small Town Girl, Corporate Affair & Keeping the Peace*
by Linda Cunningham
Stitches and Scars by Elizabeth A. Vincent
Take the Cake by Sandra Wright
Pieces of Us by Hannah Downing
The Way That You Play It by BJ Thornton
The Poughkeepsie Brotherhood series: *Poughkeepsie & Return to Poughkeepsie*
by Debra Anastasia
Cocktails & Dreams and *The Art of Appreciation* by Autumn Markus
Recaptured Dreams and *All-American Girl* and *Until Next Time* by Justine Dell
Once Upon a Second Chance by Marian Vere
The Englishman by Nina Lewis
16 Marsden Place by Rachel Brimble
Sleepers, Awake by Eden Barber
The Runaway Year by Shani Struthers
The Hydraulic series: *Hydraulic Level Five* by Sarah Latchaw
Fix You by Beck Anderson
Just Once by Julianna Keyes
The WORDS series: *The Weight of Words & Better Deeds Than Words* by Georgina Guthrie
Theatricks by Eleanor Gwyn-Jones
The Sacrificial Lamb by Elle Fiore
The Plan by Qwen Salsbury
The Kiss Me series: *Kiss Me Goodnight & Kiss Me by Moonlight* by Michele Zurlo
Saint Kate of the Cupcake: The Dangers of Lust and Baking by LC Fenton
Exposure by Morgan & Jennifer Locklear
Playing All the Angles by Nicole Lane

New Adult Romance

Three Daves by Nicki Elson
Streamline by Jennifer Lane
The Shades series: *Shades of Atlantis & Shades of Avalon* by Carol Oates
The Heart series: *Beside Your Heart, Disclosure of the Heart & Forever Your Heart*
by Mary Whitney
Romancing the Bookworm by Kate Evangelista
The Fate series: *Fighting Fate* by Linda Kage
Flirting with Chaos by Kenya Wright
The Vice, Virtue & Video series: *Revealed & Captured* by Bianca Giovanni

Young Adult Romance

The Ember series: *Ember & Iridescent* by Carol Oates
Breaking Point by Jess Bowen
Life, Liberty, and Pursuit by Susan Kaye Quinn
The Embrace series: *Embrace & Hold Tight* by Cherie Colyer
Destiny's Fire by Trisha Wolfe
The Reaper series: *Reaping Me Softly & UnReap My Heart* by Kate Evangelista
The Legendary Saga: *Legendary* by LH Nicole
Fatal by T.A. Brock

Paranormal Romance

The Light series: *Seers of Light, Whisper of Light & Circle of Light* by Jennifer DeLucy
The Hanaford Park series: *Eve of Samhain & Pleasures Untold* by Lisa Sanchez
Immortal Awakening by KC Randall
The Seraphim series: *Crushed Seraphim & Bittersweet Seraphim* by Debra Anastasia
The Guardian's Wild Child by Feather Stone
Grave Refrain by Sarah M. Glover
Divinity by Patricia Leever
Blood Vine series: *Blood Vine, Blood Entangled & Blood Reunited* by Amber Belldene
Divine Temptation by Nicki Elson
Love in the Time of the Dead by Tera Shanley

Historical Romance

Cat O' Nine Tails by Patricia Leever
Burning Embers by Hannah Fielding
Good Ground by Tracy Winegar

Romantic Suspense

Whirlwind by Robin DeJarnett
The CONduct series: *With Good Behavior, Bad Behavior & On Best Behavior*
by Jennifer Lane
Indivisible by Jessica McQuinn
Between the Lies by Alison Oburia
Blind Man's Bargain by Tracy Winegar

Erotic Romance

The Keyhole series: *Becoming sage* (book 1) by Kasi Alexander
The Keyhole series: *Saving sunni* (book 2) by Kasi & Reggie Alexander
The Winemaker's Dinner: *Appetizers & Entrée* by Dr. Ivan Rusilko & Everly Drummond
The Winemaker's Dinner: *Dessert* by Dr. Ivan Rusilko
Client N° 5 by Joy Fulcher

coming soon from
OMNIFIC PUBLISHING

The Prometheus Order series: *Byronic* (book 1) by Sandi Beth Jones
One Smart Cookie by Kym Brunner
The Vice, Virtue & Video series: *Desired* (book 3) by Bianca Giovanni
Seven for a Secret by Rumer Haven
Skygods by Sarah Latchaw
Loving Lies by Linda Kage

www.ingramcontent.com/pod-product-compliance
Lightning Source LLC
Chambersburg PA
CBHW020522120726

47904CB00003B/931